Life of a Military Psychologist
A Story of Tragedy and Spiritual Awakening

A Novel

by

Sally Wolf, PhD

For permission, serialization, condensation, adaptions, or for our catalog of other publications, write to Ozark Mountain Publishing, Inc., P.O. Box 754, Huntsville, AR 72740, ATTN: Permissions Department.

Library of Congress Cataloging-in-Publication Data

Sally Wolf -1953-

Life of a Military Psychologist by Sally Wolf

With the stock market tanking, Dr. Sara is forced from her comfortable small town therapy practice and thrust into the violent world of military mental health and intimate partner violence.

1. Mental Health 2. War 3. Metaphysical 4. Therapy
I. Sally Wolf, 1953, 1958 II. Metaphysical III.Therapy IV. Title

Library of Congress Catalog Card Number: 2021942518
ISBN: 9781950639076

Cover Art and Layout: Victoria Cooper Art
Book set in: Multiple Fonts
Book Design: Summer Garr
Published by:

PO Box 754, Huntsville, AR 72740
800-935-0045 or 479-738-2348; fax 479-738-2448
WWW.OZARKMT.COM

Printed in the United States of America

Contents

———◇———

Nov. 5, 2009, 1:34 p.m.

Rivers of sweat run down the temples of the dark-eyed army major. He is large and sweating like fat men sweat—deliberately and without restraint. He says nothing as he lumbers into the Fort Hood Deployment Readiness Center. Glancing to left and right, he ignores the pleasant greetings military and civilian workers are required to offer. Major Hasan stalks past silently, his lips pursed, responding to the voices only he can hear. He disregards those who salute him as he pushes through the crowd. His booted stride is long and purposeful; he moves to the center of the waiting room filled with deploying men and women and commandeers a metal chair and wooden desk. Drip. He sits down hard in the chair; his belly pushes out of his pants over the top of his belt; his pockets bulge. His breathing is labored; his head juts forward and his eyes slant down to the table, staring blankly into the marred wood. Drip. Drip. The sweat drops onto the table with his muttered words, drowned out by Readiness Center chatter. Fluid streams down his chin, forming droplets pooling on the table beneath his bowed head. His mumbled words cease.

Shots ring out.

Drip. Drip.

i

Chapter One

---◆---

Voices

November 5, 2009, 1:34 p.m.

It is sweating hot, unseasonably hot for a November in Oceanside, California. My clothes cling to me; I feel the wetness under my knees. As a psychologist for the Marine Corps base counseling services I am using the office no one else wants to use. It is a closet-sized space with no windows, no ventilation, but lots of heat, resulting in uncomfortable squirming by the domestic violence (DV) offender I am interviewing. We are about halfway through his offender assessment. I ask him to verify the details of his assault on his wife that are referred to in the police report. I push the police report schema of the female anatomy toward him over the desk. It is marked in several places indicating injuries from the trauma he has inflicted on his spouse. The markings on this female outline are drawn in short staccato strokes that give hints of the impact of the intimate partner rage. Our imaginations do the rest. The image comes alive as we review the etched scratches from his bitten nails that jaggedly dug into the thin skin of her forehead. A blue pen mark shows the discoloration on the victim's neck from the strangulation that could have ended her life. A black dot punches up the eye injury designation to the female drawing. A smudge like a semicolon on the edge of the womanly outline signposts an excreted fluid. I can almost taste the blood that seeped from this victim's mouth, and I wince at the evidence of the pain from an eye socket so swollen the victim could not see. The uniformed offender looks away from the illustration, his eyes following an ant on the side of the wall. His words dodge and weave, denying everything, and insisting he is the real victim. His lies are as clear as his discomfort from the heat. In this closed room, his body odor smells of alcohol from the night before and tobacco from heavy smoking. Water beads up around the transparent cowlick on the brow of his shaven head. The tattoo at the base of his neck is a sickly blue color with crossed swords and a skull staring back at me with sunken eyes. We both notice it is fatally hot, and if we agree on only one thing in this session it is that I should do something about the sweltering closeted heat before someone passes out.

I did not seek out domestic violence counseling. I didn't find this job as a civilian psychologist for the military; it found me. The work is thankless, sad, and generally unrewarding. The economy drove me into military service, much as it does for young teens fresh from the most rural parts of America. Each day brings new kids to me; offender and victim stories are always the same. Violence. Pain. Lost honor. Disgrace. I see this cycle of power and control repeated over and over when victims refuse to leave their attackers and attackers refuse to be accountable for their actions.

I came here late in my career. I moved to San Diego following my heart and built a private practice that fell with the DOW. I found myself working pro bono in a world that still required me to pay. Without abandoning my practice and the patients who relied on me, I moved into the military world, believing I could make a positive contribution and continue what I had built in reputation, respect, and self-satisfaction.

I was hired to do trauma response work and general counseling, but the funding shifted, and all trauma therapists had to add domestic violence cases to their work. The military violent offender program is called "Family Advocacy"—newspeak for berating, humiliating, beating, or maiming an intimate partner or child. Some think military culture breeds this behavior. Some studies suggest that when your principal job is to kill, such incidents are also more likely within intimate partnerships. Military culture is violent and rigid by nature. The mix of multiple deployments, post-traumatic stress disorder (PTSD), collisions of personal beliefs, sex role stereotyping, and returning home to children who are virtual strangers can lead to escalated conflicts.

These very young people simply don't know how to resolve heated disagreements with words; they are physical by nature and violent by training. They use physical engagement or destroying things to express their feelings. It isn't until domestic violence offenders are arrested or brought in to family advocacy by Commands, like this guy in front of me, that they hear that such behavior is abusive. Most grew up acting out verbally and physically even before they joined up. They call it "venting."

Military training can lend deadly force to domestic violence acts. A good example is the guy I am sitting with inside this closed-door cooker; a rear bare-naked choke hold becomes an expedient way to get your spouse in line and make her do what you want. Such beliefs as "A woman should always do what a man says" or "A woman should not have male friends" can justify the physical restraint and injury of spouses. Sometimes military offenders confess they have harmed their spouse's beloved pet. This falls along the spectrum of emotional abuse, which can take many forms within the military community, such as intimidation, stalking, demeaning by hurtful words, or denying a spouse access to benefits and services on the base.

This guy's wife is really scared. She hid her black eye under layers of foundation, and she tied a scarf around her neck over the ligature marks before she met with the victim advocate. She just won't return calls now. Her loving husband sitting in front of me was lying when he said nothing happened, but challenging him, interrogating him will do little more than provoke him. Neither of us wants that. Hammering on him won't result in a sudden epiphany in which he sees the light, says he is sorry, and asks for help. That doesn't happen except on television. He sits slumped in the chair, uttering grunting noises and making up stories as to how his wife might have gotten those marks on her neck. He uses four-letter words to paint a picture of her clumsiness and her inability to keep it together. His ultimate verdict is that she is "a crazy bitch who makes stuff up just to get him in trouble." We go through the motions of an interview like a ceremonial dance, where he lies, and I listen and we both lose. Whether he cops to it or not, he will be thrown into a cookie-cutter offender group for sixteen weeks in a system where tattling, busted jaws, and bent bones become data points dumped into the military offender registry.

Completed intervention and rehabilitation are rare.

Offender group facilitators come in with strong motives to help but are rebuffed continuously and eventually leave with unacknowledged compassion fatigue and no help along the way from the administration. The facilitators jockey for position among the leadership hierarchy, hoping to become one of the chosen few who get a better office and a decent parking space. Marine Corps base Camp Pendleton has the largest number of offender groups in the entire Marine Corps.

Being shut into this tiny stifling room has become unbearable. I politely (it is always important to be polite with a violent offender) excuse myself and set off to find the thermostat switch to kick on the air conditioner. I look about, but I can't find it. I feel like I have been working here forever, and yet the little things, like not knowing where the thermostat is, remind me of how draining this place can be in a short time.

I make my way down the corridor lined with the offices of clinicians, victim advocates, and old-timers. Here offices are assigned by two factors: how long you have worked here and your rank among the manager's favorites. Nepotism is rampant; professionalism is nil. Those needing confidential spaces for professional business are often left with limited or no privacy. People stay here long past their desire to be here. They are burned out to the core but are afraid to leave the perceived financial security of this soul-killing atmosphere. I find myself becoming jaded, losing the optimism and spiritual outlook I have been known for throughout my life. I miss that part of me.

The counseling services manager rushes around the corner and almost bumps into me. She is wearing tiny pointed heels that make a clacking sound even on carpet. The manager for nine years, she is difficult to read. Her sly Cheshire cat smile is her uniform, and she spends her days asserting her will at random. To need to be so much in control, she must really be scared. I look her over as we go toe-to-toe. She is wearing a crisply ironed blouse, slim skirt, and nylon stockings. She prefers that all female staff wear pantyhose, but in this heat, she has chosen for herself not to fight that battle. Her hair is properly dyed, and her shoes are properly closed at the toes.

She maintains her smile as she stands at attention in front of me. I am careful whenever I talk to her because I know I might be blindsided by a demeaning remark packaged in a pleasant tone and delivered with a smile.

"Sarah, I'm glad I ran into you"—she laughs at her joke. "I had to break into your office earlier."

Okay, it has happened again, I am caught off guard. I have trained myself to always reply positively. My faith begs me to remain positive and hopeful, always respectful of authority. I know I should send this woman love, not harbor anger because it will only come back to hurt me. However, in my human consciousness, I am thinking, "What the hell?"

"That's okay," I muster. "You are always welcome to go into my office; you don't have to call it breaking in, what did you need?"

"Sarah, you gave the credential renewal office copies of two professional licenses you have, as well as all of your credentials as college teacher, college counselor, and more after that."

"Ma'am, I did do that. They asked for copies of all my credentials and professional licenses, and I have my licenses posted in my office per Marine Corps protocol. What is the problem?"

"Sarah, I had to take time to break into your office

to find a single copy of your license. You submitted two license copies posted on one sheet."

"Ma'am, if you want one license on each paper, just fold the paper and copy the license you have in your hand onto one sheet. You really didn't need to break in. I was here interviewing an offender in a different office while they cleaned my office. You could have asked me."

She cut me off, "Did you want something else?" She has mastered the art of dismissing staff in the quickest and "friendliest" way. She has her own style of micromanagement whimsy.

With her break-in declared, and her desire to dismiss me apparent, I know I must make my request known before she clicks and clacks off down the hall. I ask her where to find the thermostat temperature controls. The reason for my asking should be obvious. Apparently, it is not. In the next moments I pray a silent prayer and cling quietly to my sane and reasonable perceptions. My inner voice must suffice for a reality check. My professional perspective, which has been long trusted and respected throughout my career, has no place in the cronyism of counseling services.

The manager motions for me to come with her outside the building, and at first, I think we are on a journey to get the cool air happening, so I can resume my busy work with the menacing uniformed offender in my office. Perhaps the controls are outside. My ardent desire for relief and my naive assumption of her cooperation give me an overly optimistic view of the future. As we make our way outside and onto a rickety wooden ramp, the manager stops suddenly, turning her short, diminutive frame, and points to the large air-conditioning unit sitting directly behind the building. She teeters for a moment on her elevated stilettos.

She sticks out her brown freckled finger, pointing to the air conditioner, and asks me, "Do you know what that is?"

I have no idea where she is going with this, and I wonder if it's one of her rambling, diatribe moments the other counselors whisper about. The manager continues in a directional pose, her arm quivering with military rigidity. I need to get back to the offender, so I simply shake my head, indicating I have no idea what she means. This is not a small moment; she thinks I am supposed to be impressed by her dominance. This is power and control pure and simple and it feels like crap. She insists on going further, "The very unit I am pointing to is controlled by me, and you have no control of it now and will not have any control of it later. There will be no changing the thermostat."

I feel my mouth wanting to drop into a gape, but I hold on to it. This is business as usual at counseling services. The most painful aspect of working with the military is surviving the civilian-led administration, not the secondary trauma we endure with our patients.

The manager is clearly "Queen" of this moment, and although my gut twists, there is no opportunity for my response. Silence is the preferred employee communication. Counselors talk so much about nonverbal communication in counseling sessions, but here inequity and management dysfunction hang silently in each room like curtains drawn to keep out new thoughts and shutters sealed tight to hold in family advocacy secrets and hold onto old, ineffective but familiar routines.

As I walk away, she reminds me to be at the auditorium in the 13 Area no later than 1800. I wave my hand over my head in acknowledgment and grunt out an "oo-rah!" Oo-rah is the utterance of choice in the Marine

Corps to punctuate almost anything positive or negative, rendered from low to high volume. The domestic violence offender and I will simply have to suffer through the rest of our assessment in an atmosphere like a sauna. Oo-rah.

Chapter Two

———◆———

Friendly Fire

Fox News is blaring in the lobby as I walk through the waiting room, beaten down and wondering how I have found myself in a place that addresses the abusive control of offenders while imposing its own abusive brand of control. I notice that breaking news has drawn everyone around the monitor to listen and watch. Something has happened. Curious, I stop to watch the news report.

"Thirteen people have been murdered at the Fort Hood Army Base in Texas this day. Witnesses report a psychiatrist, a major in the US Army, had walked into the Deployment Readiness Center at 1:34 p.m., drawn semiautomatic weapons from his officer's uniform, and walked forward firing on uniformed men and women, one of them pregnant. The major was a killing machine in motion. The Readiness Center is a busy, crowded place, the first place soldiers and civilian caregivers come after deployment and the last place soldiers and civilian medical staff visit before they deploy. One of those killed was a sixty-two-year-old physician assistant, a large man, with a booming voice and what family said was a quiet wit and a wry sense of humor. He did what he could to stop the rampaging officer but fell in the gunfire. Soldiers getting ready for deployment were shot and killed. Returning soldiers were shot and killed. By the time it was over, thirteen screaming voices were silenced forever, and thirty other service members had been wounded. Blood had stained the carpet and the stench of death and gunpowder had stained the air."

Eight of us, clinicians all, just stand there watching the news report. No one says a word. We hear about casualties in the military every day. We are kept informed of casualties in the US and in combat, and we understand the trauma that causes. We treat victims and perpetrators of violence, domestic violence, and sexual assaults concerning both male and female victims, attempted suicides, and PTSD (or as the more politically correct term has it, combat stress sufferers). So, this incident at Fort Hood isn't that unusual in terms of death, mayhem, and trauma. But it was done by one of *us*, a mental health worker on American soil, a psychiatrist sworn to heal, and so today is different for us, for me.

Often the days on a military base seem to pass with little variation from the day before—endless patients, endless pain. But on this day, I wonder if today is The Day. The Day I can't take it anymore and say that's enough. The day I just leave, walk out, say good-bye to all the patients' suffering and the constraints and idiosyncrasies of military work. I pray every day for guidance and I wonder if guidance can manifest as something so horrific that it could catapult me out instead of a long slow road to retirement.

I can hear the news report continuing to announce

the casualties at Fort Hood as I make my way back to the man I am interviewing. I decide to let the waiting service member off the hook.

"I have what I need for the day, but I'll follow up with you later," I tell him as I begin tidying up the notepads and pens scattered on the office desk. The story would remain the same, but the paperwork would need to be finished and filed before the end of the week. Filling fourteen pages of the assessment with "I didn't do it" is a lot of work. There is nothing green about doing business here. Reams of paper are gobbled up by redundant statements, resulting in more paper, more stories, and little resolution. The result for the patient doesn't matter nearly as much as that the paperwork is filed appropriately.

The manager pops into my office. She hands me a certificate she accidently scooped up when she broke in earlier. I look at its title: "Strangulation."

"Where else can you get a certificate in strangulation?" I muse.

Her smile is oddly absent. "Be at the auditorium tonight no later than 1800."

I have offered to work with the helicopter squadron on my own time tonight. She mumbles that it was indeed a tragedy, but we are thin staffed and can't help everybody. If the squadron needs more help than me doing a "grief brief," they would just have to go to the Military One Source. "There are plenty of other counselors that do just as good a job as you do, but no one else wanted to get up on this rainy night in front of so many sad people and talk about the stages of grief. A good therapist likes to work one on one."

And then she adds, "You can have a 29 card if you want but don't put in for comp time." A 29 card means you can leave twenty-nine minutes early. It is given by the manager if someone works overtime. No professional could ever leave when their work was finished or if they had a long and difficult day, but they could leave if they turned in a 29 card, doled out to favorite employees or unavoidable overtime employees who had to be compensated in some way other than a fair and proper paycheck compensation.

I acknowledge to her that I understand and that I still feel a desire to speak. I would check in with the chaplain and family readiness officer (FRO) who oversees organizing the brief tonight and coordinates family-related programs for all the squadrons that comprise the entire wing. She is on the frontline of dealing with the loss of the seven marines in the nighttime desert training accident. She is not a counselor by training but is the one that widows turn to in such situations. On the other hand, the military chaplains are used to dealing with death, pain, "mishaps," and are a comforting presence to all of us. I especially like flying for the Marine Corps with chaplains, I feel it is a tad bit safer with them by my side, especially experiencing turbulence. I thought in the past that I might be an excellent chaplain, albeit, a generic spiritual one. But those feelings have long since faded.

I walk out into the rain and quickly get into my car and turn on my CD player. The Texas twang booms through my speakers. It is Joel Osteen, the Houston pastor, telling me that this is my time, and that I can get through anything and do whatever my mind and faith inspire me to do. I need Joel Osteen. It isn't religious dogma that speaks to me but this southern drawl of generalized optimism of hope, telling me that I can get through anything and it will definitely get better. In this arena of such tragedy and loss, I am a seeker of spiritual comfort not eloquent parables or passages. However, the saying "there are no unbelievers in foxholes" also speaks to me.

My Porsche seems especially old tonight. It is pouring rain and the wipers on my 1976 912E drag across the windshield. The blades are barely moving the rain off the glass. I inch slowly around the hill from counseling services, hydroplaning as I coast down along the final stretch to the huge building at the bottom of the hill.

The large auditorium where the meeting is scheduled sits adjacent to the road that runs across the back of the base near the Naval Weapons Station. Tonight, the building is surrounded by government trucks. I pull into a compact space near the loading zone, out of the rain. I see workers unloading armfuls of folding chairs, and volunteers bringing in bottled water and snacks. Seven enlarged photos of helmeted pilots and flight-suited crew chiefs are leaning against the entrance wall under the awning. These are the victims, the strong-looking, smiling, and confident pilots and crew chiefs who were training so ferociously when they met their death.

This meeting venue had been booked for months in preparation for the helicopter assault group predeployment brief. These predeployment briefs are for all members of the squadron, including their loved ones. They review where the marines will be living and fighting in Afghanistan, and they introduce key volunteers and family readiness officers. FROs provide linkage to Command and handle all the family-related emotional and logistical issues during a deployment. These matters can include wives giving birth, either party getting in trouble, or financial issues, and in the event of a marine's death, FROs assist in spouse notification and support. FROs have no designation as counselors, but they certainly are on the frontline of face-to-face support for military families and hear all the bad news first. They often feel the brunt of extreme emotional reaction by families reeling from incidents such as the loss of these seven marines last week.

The commanding officer could not deviate from the required procedure for deployment meetings, but he did not want to simply continue training and briefing for the deployment without acknowledging the importance of paying respect to the squadron's losses and need to grieve, even if just for a moment before training continued. That would be my job tonight. I would be the bridge across the abyss. I am the one elected to comfort, to give permission to grieve, to assist those in grieving, and then to move on to the business of getting ready to leave. I am honored to meet with these valiant families. I would have half an hour to accomplish what normally takes at least a year. I feel a tightness in my chest.

It is almost unfathomable to imagine gathering a squadron of over four hundred helicopter pilots and crew with their spouses to encourage them to grieve in the same breath as telling them they must continue to train and deploy next month for Afghanistan. No wonder I feel this tightness in my chest. The rain is falling all around but I am standing still under the abutment. The wind whips the cold wet fluid onto my face and neck. It feels like small moist needles against my body. I take a long slow breath and open myself to a higher power. I know that I prepare best for a presentation when I meditate, pray, breathe, and let go. It is essential that I stay centered and know that I step in with celestial support.

These marines and their loved ones are being asked to do the impossible at this moment. They are asked to cry, but don't cry too much because you must be able to operate these complex birdlike machines like the ones that just crashed carrying your best friends and the teachers who taught you that you were invincible and would win the day if you concentrated and trained hard. No one concentrated more, knew more, or trained harder than the ones who collided with each other and by the way you must be razor sharp to engage the enemy next month and ferry your fellow marines in and out of harm's way with precision accuracy. Grief-stricken pilots must jockey their armored birds filled with fuel and loaded with the ammunition to feed those machine guns on the flank of the flying beast. You must take out the enemy that has your military brothers pinned down in the bitter cold of winter or the long suffocating summer.

It is raining hard now. The sky has opened, and I just can't bring myself to go in yet. The driveway next to the auditorium is flooding, workers are scrambling to get the huge photos of the dead inside for placement. Their helmets, flak jackets, rifles, and boots are also there, stacked over to the side. These are the items always placed in reverence at memorials. I wonder why they are here. This is not the memorial; this is the working brief. I see the workers carefully put them in locked cabinets across the back of the room for presentation at the memorial, which will happen later in the week. The tightness in my chest is familiar to me. Speaking about grief and loss brings back memories of my mother. My mother and best friend died thirty years ago, and I still miss her; grief work always rekindles past experiences of loss. I will remember to be diverse in my presentation tonight; each person in that room tonight will be feeling grief in personal and unique ways from this experience and other losses they have endured, and I must remain mindful and sensitive.

Diversity is the hallmark of my work. I offer individual counseling for active-duty military, I lead violent military offender groups, and I speak at very large military venues performing briefs at the discretion of my boss for whatever human emotion is of greatest concern at the time. The emotion might be anger related to an incident off the base. It might be sexual assault prevention following heinous acts by multiple military personnel or, occasions like tonight, when no one else at counseling services wants to step up to face the grief and offer words where words fall short. It is my privilege. It is no accident that I am here. People are entering the building now. Some have reddened eyes and are crying. Some wear military issue sunglasses in the rain. There are women in their twenties pushing baby strollers. There is childcare elsewhere, but no one is going to tell a mother she can't bring in her infant tonight. Couples hold onto each other, and single marines look around nervously; this will be their first deployment. I see the FRO standing to the side. She is well dressed, poised, and speaks in a staccato manner, punctuating each phrase with "yes, ma'am." She is a civilian but sounds like a military officer as she announces that she is grateful I am here. I respect her.

I express my condolences. I take a long and slow deep breath before I enter the building, and we walk in together. I must steel myself but remain soft to connect to feelings and emotions in the room. If I harden myself, it will be no good to anyone. Maintaining my professional and emotional balance is a challenge serving under the present counseling services management. I am called upon to do so much, rise to engage at the highest level, only to be cut down at any moment and put in a tightly controlled box. I consciously let go of any thought of the craziness at counseling services and send them love, to move into this moment. My purpose, on this inclement night, is to encourage military members and spouses to grieve at the same time they are given mind-numbing instructions for deployment at end of the month.

Marine leaders will tell the squadron and their tear-stained loved ones to train harder and get ready as they bury seven of their own from a training "mishap." The military calls the midair collision of the huge armed Cobra helicopter that was holding two senior military pilot trainers and the machine-gun-mounted Yankee helicopter, which held five in its belly, a "mishap." What a strange term. It lacks the emotion and the power of the tragedy, but perhaps that is the point. So, with the room booked, and the need to push ahead understood by all, I was elected to greet them, support them, grieve with them, and lead them into the predeployment brief. After all, everyone knows humans need to grieve for their dead, and especially for their brothers in arms. If humans don't grieve, if they hold it in, the pain oozes out without warning. Just don't grieve too much or lose your concentration when it is needed—wars dictate that. Distraction or the thought of a lost teammate can yield life-and-death split-second consequences. I play my presentation again in my head, over and over. The most structured and the best of presentations don't always flow the way you want them to when human emotion is involved.

Lieutenant Colonel Bravebull, the commanding officer and a Native American, opens the meeting. He is speaking now. It feels like slow motion as I look around the room at the morose faces and tissue-grabbing hands. Bravebull is a lean athletic man, six feet tall, dressed in his flight suit, with an energy about him that is strong and purposeful and radiates compassion and caring. He is articulate, stoic, and speaks deliberately as his words guide each of us through every hideous detail of what he describes as "the mishap." He announces that he feels that giving the details of the mishap will provide closure and answer questions regarding the incident. I can see the faces of the spouses begin to drain of color and light as he moves about the room.

"The desert night was with zero illumination. There was no moon. We train in the most remote part of the desert; night goggle vision is our only perspective because it most closely resembles where and how they will fight. We conquer the night through this training and honestly, we live for it. The Cobra and the Yankee helicopters were piloted by the best of our best." Lieutenant Colonel Bravebull speaks with resolution, but his breathing is shallow, and emotion can be heard rattling in his throat.

"The birds had just refueled and carried significant ordnance on board. When they collided, they hit so hard and fell so close together that it resulted in an inferno on the ground. Ordnance shot forth everywhere, and the fire was so intense that although fire and rescue crews rushed to the scene, they were rebuffed repeatedly." He chokes. I am keeping constant eye contact with him; I move closer and hand him a water bottle. I touch his hand; it is trembling. He continues, "The fire response crews used all of their fire-retardant foam and because of the remote location, they ran out and were unable to replenish their supply." I can hear moaning in the back of the room. He continues.

"They had to wait and watch until the fire subsided before recovering the victims." A sergeant major at the side of the auditorium gags on hearing this. Spouses bury their heads in flight crew chests. Tears fall on plastic tables and into tissues grabbed from boxes on every table.

"Because of the remote area, there was difficulty with communication. Individuals at Camp Pendleton could not get confirmed information for quite some time.

Satellite phones were the only way they were able to get information and that took hours. Loved ones were calling in asking Command why their husbands had not returned home from training. There was a delay in confirming victims, but it was necessary. I felt terrible for having to wait, but I had to get it right."

He presents a PowerPoint projected on the huge screen at the front of the auditorium. He knew each flyer personally. The six-foot images of each marine's photo and family bio are haunting. Each is smiling; each is so alive. They were fathers, sons, expectant fathers, and each has a poignant story. All the fallen marines were "extraordinary." One was a violin maker's child, a crew chief, one a musician who played the guitar, and each man loved his family and did what he loved for a living.

The four hundred fifty service members and spouses sit in absolute silence. Some get up and take their babies out of the room. None of the children makes a sound but babies serve as great excuses to escape the stories of the dead, on screen. One FRO who normally is professional and organized appears distracted and numb. She gets up suddenly, wiping her eyes, and leaves the room.

Originally, I was told I would follow the chaplain's presentation in the middle of the brief, but suddenly the lieutenant colonel simply walks over to me and hands me the microphone.

"Hello, I am Dr. Fox and, on this night, where words fall short of addressing your losses, I am here to speak to you about grief." I speak slowly with reverence and respect. I look at the colonel and his wife sitting directly in front of me and at Lieutenant Colonel Bravebull leaning back in his chair with the audience behind him. Bravebull's brow is furrowed; his eyes dart back and forth. His right fist opens and closes in a nervous gesture.

I always prepare carefully for a presentation, and this time is no different. I have no intention of using a PowerPoint, but I have bullet points to refer to, outlining stages of grief and the evolution of understanding that grief does not fit neatly into stages. However, in that moment I must leave a structured speech behind and move into the experience. A higher power steps in to replace linear notes and guide my presentation.

"Grieve, you must grieve." I nod to the colonel in the front row. "Don't hold it in." I pause and continue to move slowly, acknowledging him to the audience as well as the lieutenant colonel to punctuate the permission by leadership to mourn. "It is important to openly grieve to move through it and past it. If you don't, it will ooze out when you least want it to. There is no right way to feel it; some may cry openly; others may want to use sunglasses to veil their pain. Join with each other and respect each other's process in grieving; it will be unique to each of you.

"It may feel like a wave taking you over without notice, or a song, a smell, or a taste of food that reminds you of your brothers lost and your loved ones gone. Be gentle with each other; reach out to each other and know that you will get through this in time."

I look at the chaplain and stretch out my hand to him. "This is the time you call upon your faith and allow yourself to accept help from those who offer and from the Greater Power that you connect with in the privacy of your mind and soul." I touch on the grief stages and talk about what they may feel, such as numbness, isolation, denial, or anger.

I know I must give them something more. They all look disconnected, numb and cut off from feelings. I must give them something they can grab onto, something that will help them connect to feelings and ground them. If I just talk at them and lecture them, they will never forgive me, and I will not forgive myself. So, I go there with them. I dare to tempt their grief to come out.

"If you will join me, take your right hand and lay it across your heart, breathing deeply and slowly." I grasp my chest and meet them where they are in pain.

"Do you feel like you have been kicked in the gut? Lay your arm across your stomach. If you feel your heart is literally, physically breaking lay your hand on your heart, and if you feel you are choked with your feelings, lay your hand on your throat."

I invite them to imagine being grounded there so they can breathe through it, breathe into it.

"If you feel too much, ground yourself and let it out slowly. The fear is that if you really tap into it and let it out, it will overpower you. The opposite is true. Relief, even for a moment, acts as a sluice valve to let grief out and foster healing."

I continue by reiterating that each person has a distinctive experience, and although it may look like they are not outwardly showing grief, it does not mean they are grieving less, just differently. I confirm that our counselors will be coming to their location to work one on one with anyone who needs it. I give counseling services screening hours.

Knowing that the squadron has to move on to their predeployment brief, I end my presentation with a kinesthetic anchoring technique that I can teach them easily.

"Think of a time … this is for everyone … think of a time before the mishap when you could concentrate. Imagine yourself for just a moment as confident, focused, and razor sharp. Hold that positive and powerful thought. Firmly touch your forefinger to your thumb and hold it tightly with that thought." I held my connected thumb and forefinger high in the air, so they could see. "With practice, this anchor will empower you to do what you need to do, when you need to do it."

The chaplain jumps up and thanks me, dismissing everyone for a twenty-minute break before the predeployment meeting. Lieutenant Colonel Bravebull tells me that it was just what they wanted, and he adds that he especially appreciates my ending with a positive anchoring technique, which they will use.

Many people take our cards and tell me they prefer to ask questions privately. The FRO asks if I will speak to their monthly meeting. I tell her I will put that request forward, and it would be my pleasure. But I know I will have no control over whether I will be allowed to go.

There will be more tomorrow, and tomorrow.

Chapter Three

---◆---

Tomorrow

There are over 80,000 people on Camp Pendleton on any given day here in Oceanside, and in the early morning we all squish together in congested merging lanes to gain entrance to the base. As I drive in, I listen to National Public Radio and feel moved by a radio interview with a journalist who was tortured and detained in Iran for months. Emotion tightens my throat as he speaks. He says it wasn't a traditional torture, like being deafened by blared music or sleep deprivation; it wasn't even advanced interrogation like water-boarding. What almost destroyed him was being told daily that his work was nothing, that what he did didn't matter and that he was alone, that they could do whatever they wanted to him or discard him like he was nothing, that his life had no meaning. His captors gnawed away at his self-esteem, his ability to feel good about himself, the value of his contribution, his profession, and his self-perception. It wasn't the physical pain; it was the emotional anguish. It's odd because DV victims say the same thing. What stays with humans is how they are

24

treated and abused over time, not one defining physical incident.

As I hear the journalist on the radio speak, I feel a kinship with him; I know in my bones what he means. I am only two years into serving as a therapist on base; many of my co-workers have been here years longer and have aged prematurely. For me the pain is in the awareness of moving from the respect of being Dr. Fox—with all the clinical prowess that implies—to a name tag declaring my first name, Sarah. I often feel like asking if someone would like French fries with their appointment. Being a licensed clinician and trained trauma therapist seems to mean nothing, garner no respect. The overly familiar name tags were the manager's decision to make patients feel more comfortable in a situation where the stigma is palpable in the waiting room. The need to impose subordination by the management is in tune with the military practice of breaking individuals down in boot camp to form them back up in the role that is required of them, stripping their uniqueness and their own personality from them for the greater good. While perhaps this method works in creating the perfect military fighter, in a therapeutic environment it leads to a soul-crushing experience for the clinician. This is the climate that the massacring major worked within at Fort Hood.

Perhaps such an environment sows seeds that lead to mental breakdown, to unleashing desperate acts. Reporters said the major at Fort Hood kept trying to tell everyone he couldn't deploy again, that he just couldn't do it. But in a military environment, the Command control is paramount and listening to what someone can't do, even an officer, is never tolerated. On the other hand, in a world of liberating a country, storming Fallujah, or holding the line in the face of unyielding enemies, violence is expected.

In a military counseling center, we know that service members are trained to compartmentalize feelings in combat because it is essential for survival, but after theater it is imperative to talk about it, not keep it inside, and to get help if it is needed. In the case of the good doctor at Fort Hood, he appears to have found his voice, screamed to the highest authority, but had to get in line and accomplish the mission. Nothing is done to address compassion fatigue and mental health workers' need to take care of themselves to operate effectively.

The media is growing the story about the major. The focus is now on the fact that he was Muslim and a terrorist. He was known to communicate with radical Islamic clerics, and according to Fox News, which is the only station we can watch at counseling services, he has "mysteriously" sent money to Pakistan. He is also now reported to be paralyzed from the neck down. It is a bit ironic that it was a woman—a civilian—who took him down by shooting him four times. But I wonder if the "Islamic thing" wasn't what totally caused the massacre at all. What if he heard just one too many stories, like each of us here at the counseling center, every day? The major was a psychiatrist at Walter Reed, so he heard the worst patient reports—the severed limbs from improvised explosive devices (IEDs), the blown-off heads from sniper fire, PTSD nightmares—and what if he just couldn't deploy, what if the horror, the shattered lives and warped after-lives got to him and he snapped, went postal in a military world? It could happen again.

As I sit here musing in the traffic, I notice this street is jammed with cars following dangerously close behind each other, driven by drivers who are so aggressive that it looks like each vehicle is trying to accomplish its own landing assault mission. Some vehicles lurch forward antagonistically, not letting other cars merge from adjacent streets. Most of the vehicles are large—trucks and muscle cars. My old Porsche is sandwiched between a lifted Ford F-250 adorned with skulls and marine logos and an old Jeep Wrangler with music blaring the whining lyrics of country music. I feel appropriately intimated, surrounded by marines whose urgent mission is to get to work by 0600. It feels like do or die.

Coming from Fallbrook I must first cross the Naval Weapons Station before entering Camp Pendleton Marine Base. As the vehicles slowly approach the entrance gate, I extend my arm from the car window and hold my military identification card out for view. Remember we are at war; the guard stands rigid at the entrance with his right hand jutted straight out in front of his body, signaling me to stop. His left hand is extended from his side in an odd horizontal fashion as if he intends to make a left turn. He wants each vehicle to pull up directly in front of his left hand. He won't look at a driver's ID card unless the car has stopped at just the right place. I inch up, and he motions for me to continue forward to the exact spot adjacent to his protruded hand. He looks like a rigid cardboard cut-out figure, standing straight and tall with one arm extended. I come through here every day, often with the same guard at the ready, and yet he always frowns and acts as if he has never seen me before. Stopping me is as important and urgent as the day before. We are at war and if by some conspiracy this is the day I choose to become a terrorist agent rather than the psychologist I claimed to be yesterday, the gate guard would be the one to hold his position and take me down. Commercial trucks are pulled over to the side of this parade with dogs sniffing around their tires, mirrors being held underneath. The welcome mat of the military is oddly unwelcoming.

After I move through the Naval Weapons gate, traffic virtually disappears; the long stretch of road before me winds through the hills and breaks free of the war zone mentality. The scenery is quite lovely: hawks fly high above, coyotes run off into the distance, and wildflowers dot the grass-covered ordnance bunkers where cows graze on the green—a landscape of open space in an otherwise regimented and controlled world. The Naval Weapons area appears vast and empty because everything is underground. The two-lane road winds over the buried ordnance bunkers on through another unmanned gate and onto the marine base.

I look over to the left as I enter Camp Pendleton, and I notice the platoon formations standing at attention on the grassy areas dotting the landscape of the old buildings. Enlisted personnel run in step along the streets, young men with shaven heads walk with rifles on their backs, and others work out by hoisting batteries over their heads and running with huge poles on their shoulders.

Out of the corner of my eye I see several women making their way through an obstacle course and onto a prescribed run. Each female marine's body type is different. A long lean woman takes one stride for every two of the short, rounded girl running next to her. I say girl because she looks no older than seventeen. Her face is flushed, and the tight bun stuck to her head, plastered by some cheap gel, makes her look like a porcelain doll.

I know that girl with the sweet porcelain doll look. She is Corporal Novak. I can't believe she is out running. She was referred to me before her surgery. She had injured her hip in a Humvee rollover accident a year ago. The poor girl had just come from boot camp back east where all the women must train. She had been trained as an avionics repairperson but on the way to the range for pistol qualification during a freak rainstorm the Humvee had overturned and pinned her underneath. A canister broke free within the vehicle and lodged against her right hip, breaking it in two places. She came in to see me utterly defeated, in pain, and discouraged at the apparent loss of her dream of being one of the few and the proud. It turns out she was escaping a family where put-downs and discouragement were the norm; she was in the Marine Corps to prove herself to an alcoholic dad and an abusive mother who projected their inadequacies and dull existence onto their daughter. With this injury and her fear of returning home, Velma felt that she had caused all of it and thought she was somehow fulfilling the negative destiny that had been perpetuated by her family. After about three weeks of eye movement desensitization and response (EMDR) therapy she was able to separate her fate from her parents' broken life. She let go of her intrusive childhood memories and moved into creating her own life of possibility. She recovered from surgery and began a physical therapy regime to reengage with her Command. It was good to see her out and about, but I hoped she wouldn't overdo it and reinjure herself.

These young women are referred to my counseling office with torn muscles, damaged shoulders, permanently injured hips—and crushed spirits. Velma has been fortunate to be able to heal and go back to work. Sometimes injuries don't heal, and women military members become mired in denial of the long-term consequences of such abuse to the female anatomy. Motivation and oo-rahs can't make up for lasting injuries.

I meet with these injured young military women, offer a safe place for them to shed the tears that leak out through their armor, and then give them support during the medical separation process. This is the dark side of the notion of *honor, courage, and commitment*—when a marine is discarded like a used-up resource that is no longer useful and soon forgotten.

Marine Corps base Camp Pendleton is adjoined by sleepy little Fallbrook village to the east, where avocados and oranges grow along sloping hillsides and the average resident is over fifty. Oceanside, to the south of Camp Pendleton, is a small coastal town that saw its peak in the surfer days of the sixties. The town is littered with bars where marines often get in trouble on leave.

I steer my old Porsche into the counseling services parking lot. Among the other cars it stands out in its austerity—practical, but small, comfortable, but not showy. Prying myself from the car is tough. My four-foot, eleven-inch frame requires that I put the seat up all the way next to the steering wheel, so I can reach the pedals, and getting out without falling on my face is a challenge. I grab my briefcase and proceed to the counseling services building, turn the keys in several locks on the door, and disarm the alarm.

I walk down a long drab corridor and unlock my office. I can see the clock above the door illuminating military time, 0600, and I sigh and put my smart card into my computer. A warning and a Department of Defense (DOD) screen saver appears, and a reminder comes up, "We are at security level 5. Do not leave your smart card in your computer and never let strangers into the building. Check IDs always. This is a high security message from Marine Headquarters." Ah, the loving embrace of Big Brother reminding me that I'm being watched.

I settle into my office and pull up my e-mail. I can't access my personal e-mail on Gmail or Yahoo; I can only use my USMC e-mail, and all my e-mail on a military installation is screened, with most Internet sites blocked.

My one escape, however, is a travel website that isn't blocked, theoretically to offer us the opportunity to book flights for government-related travel. I spend distracting moments on travel sites dreaming of where I can go to help myself remain one of the decent people. Will it be Hawaii today? Madagascar? Maybe later, but for now I put my cell phone on my desk, my only tether to the outside world.

A text message pops up from NCIS SAM. A morning pleasantry he sends each day to start *my* day. It reads: "Hello gorgeous, don't let those Fappers get you down; you are an angel amidst those demons." Fappers refers to domestic violence offenders in the Family Advocacy Program or (FAP) and the Fappers, as they are privately referred to, are the violent offenders that harm their spouses or injure their children. Sam is a very special man. For being an NCIS special agent, he remains loving and sensitive. That is surprising considering the heinous acts he has witnessed and investigated. We certainly see a side of humanity that most people turn away from in disgust. I really like this guy, but he is somewhat GUD, or geographically undesirable. He is East Coast, while my feet are firmly planted on the West Coast. I put on my reading glasses, turn on the ambient lighting and put my relaxation CD in my player while I access the myriad e-mails that greet me every morning.

Chapter Four

---◆---

The Mysterious Marine Opens Up

The first e-mail I pull up is a particularly interesting one:

> *Sending new patient over today, high security clearance, evaluation needed ASAP, critical, multiple deployments possible "combat stress," fitness for duty eval.*
>
> *V/R Commander Watkins*

V/R means very respectfully. It is how all officers sign their e-mails and how I do, too. It is odd that someone would be sent to counseling services for a "fitness for duty" mental health evaluation; we are the stepchild of clinical work at the base. Naval medicine at the mental health unit (MHU) is the big dog on base and does most, if not all "valid" evaluations; the hospital clinicians believe they are the only mental health providers on base that can accomplish adequate psych evaluations. The problem is, it is tough to get seen there. Even if you are suicidal, and I mean ready to cut, shoot, or hang yourself, they are known simply to ask you—after you have been sitting in the waiting room for five hours—if you are really sure you want to kill yourself, and anybody after sitting for five hours will generally say no just to get the hell out of there, and either do the deed or find relief at having gotten away from that sterile, condescending, cold, and judgmental clinic. Almost no service member wants to go to the mental health unit. We are a soft handshake of a clinical counseling center compared to them. Our offices have some semblance of comfort. We have moved away from the sterile hospital atmosphere to art on the walls, comfortable chairs, and we have air conditioning—when it kicks on, but no, we can't turn it on ourselves apparently.

I start drifting away again, thinking about the major at Fort Hood who killed all those people. I wonder if he was a terrorist or a victim of extreme compassion fatigue, with other predispositions that no one caught. It feels like this story has gotten through my armor, the shield that I put on every day to be able to do the work I do. I have my self-care strategy of identifying my vulnerability to a trauma that can impact how I feel and my ability to do what I do without it polluting family and friend relationships. Secondary trauma or compassion fatigue creeps up on all of us who work with domestic violence and hear battlefield stories. Military amputees recite their play-by-play stories of IED atrocities. The visual images that these stories conjure can turn into clinician nightmares, and counselors can find themselves slipping away from friends and family into intrusive thoughts, hypervigilant postures, and emotional reactions. Loved ones, who don't know what the therapist has been hearing, are left in the dark and can feel like communication breakdowns are their fault. If families only knew what clinicians are exposed to … .

I wonder from time to time about what it will look like for me personally to end my service to this ugly side of the military community. Everyone knows you can never get fired. You can be treated horribly, you can be demoted, or you can even be stripped of your office and anything that feels comfortable while continuing to serve at the Marine Corps counseling services, but you could probably die in your job.

As for me, I don't think I will end my service because of the corrosive creep of accumulated patient suffering and professional abuse. I think ending my service will have to come from something big, some horrific demon unleashed to face me down, hang over me in such a way that I just turn and walk away softly. Not from fear, but from a Greater Power, a spiritual awakening within that guides me to do what is best for me. I have always been the David to the military trauma Goliath. But that day, whenever it comes, would be the day that I choose not to fight. Each day that I set foot on the base I contemplate whether today will be the day.

The phone rings, a polite receptionist reports that there is an escorted service member in the lobby.

As I walk out of my office and lock the door behind me, I realize I have left my smart card in the computer, and my office could be accessed, and the card would be confiscated, which would leave me without access to the military base, access to my office, or access to my computer. I whirl around to go back in and grab it and nearly crash into the wall, a clumsy maneuver which must have looked fabulous on the videotape that continuously records our movement in the hallways. Sometimes I can't help but feign flashing the camera, another way I break up the seriousness of the day. I unlock the door, walk back in.

The computer screen has already changed to a huge red alert message announcing the smart card was left in the computer and is now unattended in violation. I grab the card out of its slot and hurry out of the room.

As I make my way down the hall to the front of the building, I meet two armed guards standing much too close to a sergeant in the middle; he is in uniform, staring at the floor with his shaved head hanging low. He is about six feet, three inches tall, lanky, and tapping his foot, which looks very hard to do standing in such a rigid position.

"You gentlemen are relieved; I can take it from here," I say with my usual doctor bravado.

"Begging your pardon, ma'am, but our orders are to accompany the service member everywhere, including your office." The lance corporal's words are curt, matter-of-fact but not harsh, not meant to intimidate or cause trouble. Those are his orders. He stands at attention, but not in an aggressive manner.

"I see, we do serve Command. Come with me."

They follow down the hallway back to my office; I open the door and they start to enter the room. "Stop, you stay here; you can sit next to the door in the hallway, but you are not entering my office. I am the clinician here and this is my domain. Do we understand each other? There is no other exit, so you can be sure that this is secure; the window doesn't open. And he isn't armed, is he?" My words are sharp and linger, hanging in the air. The two armed guards shake their heads and look at each other in dismay.

"Yes, ma'am," the largest lance corporal says in a resigned tone. They pull two chairs from the staff lounge near the office, and as the door closes behind me and my patient, I hear them place the chairs directly against the door. These guys are called "chasers"; let's hope it doesn't come to that today. I bring the young man in and turn to look at him. He is emaciated, gaunt; his face is sunken with depression, but his eyes are alert. He turns his gaze directly at me.

"Sorry about that," I explain. "I have to get all up in their faces to be respected and understood. I want you to feel relaxed and comfortable here; it is safe except for several caveats. Your name is Sergeant Miller; is that right?"

"Yes, I am Sergeant Miller," he says in a quiet voice.

"Okay, Sergeant Miller. It's nice to meet you. I will explain everything as we go, and I will tell you everything I am writing down."

I begin taking notes on a yellow legal pad, sitting in the less-than-comfortable tan chair across from the sergeant.

"I tell you what I am writing because people come in here apprehensive and concerned about their careers and privacy, and I figure if I do that it might put them at ease; at least that is what I would like someone to do for me. Understood?"

"Yes, ma'am, I mean, yes, doctor, I mean ... doc," he stutters.

I move closer to him. "I am going to go over informed consent first. This is what everyone should do with you; demand it if you are sent to see anyone else in a position like mine. My goal for you is that you feel more at ease here. This is probably the only place on the base where people can come and just let down a bit. However, there are some exceptions. Even if we are meeting on a federal military installation, if you see a counselor or psychologist anywhere in California and you share knowledge of abuse of any child or disabled adult or elder, then I must breach confidentiality and report it to keep them safe. In addition, if you come in depressed, I will help you, refer you for meds if you like, but if you tell me you are going to kill yourself, I must keep you safe and get you to the hospital. If you tell me you are going to kill someone else, I must breach confidentiality due to the Tarasoff Act. I must do these things. Understood?"

"Yes," he responds. He is quiet, but his eyes dart around nervously.

"Because we are on a military installation there are a couple of other elements in addition to what I just said that you need to know. If you come in and report any criminal activity, any domestic violence, any illegal substance abuse or alcohol abuse, that must be reported to Command because it is a determinate of fitness for duty. Because of the multiple deployments this is critical ..."

I must tell him these things, but I know it's tedious, I think to myself.

"Oh, let me just cut to the chase. We are at war, and if you are in any way a danger to yourself or others, unstable, addicted, or harming your family, Command wants to know. It seems they are especially interested in you. So, whether you are a spook or whatever your military occupational service or your job is, they want to know if you are fit to go, if you can keep secrets or if you could lose it."

"Yes, ma'am," he responds curtly, without looking me in the eyes but with clear alertness. He has avoided making eye contact the entire time.

"Do you have any questions about what I just said, or do you want to report anything related to the items I just reviewed with you?"

"No. No, ma'am."

"So, why did they want me to see you, Sergeant Miller, so early this morning? I must do a domestic violence offender group in a little while, and I am not quite sure what to do with you. Why are you really here?" I sit back and catch his gaze, and we simply look at each other. I break the contact first.

"I see in the paperwork the guard gave me that you were in Haditha, Fallujah, Kirkuk, and Mosul in 2004–2005. God, what a time to be in all those places! And then TQ Ramadi 2006–2007, Baghdad 2008–2009, is that correct?" Astonishing. Those times and places were hit the hardest—this man has seen some shit. He nods his head and I continue.

"Were you ever blown up?" I ask, as I always do when meeting a postdeployment service member. I say it as a matter of routine. An affirmative response is almost guaranteed.

He suddenly blurts out, "Yes, repeatedly, but back then no one even talked about it, no treatment; you just lived with the ringing in the ears, the headaches, the joint problems! My knees are blown out, my shoulder when the Humvee flipped and landed upside down is still hurt but I just go on; I don't want to go up on Medical Boards; I am in it for another twenty years, I hope."

"Do you have any ringing in the ears or hearing issues now?" I ask. So many locations for that period of time seems odd. Usually one or two, but all those places during the height of war is out of place.

"Please don't … don't tell, ma'am. I want to stay in, and you know what they do; you do your job; your body takes a beating, and then they just get rid of you, especially those grunts. Man, their backs, shoulders, knees, and their minds are totally blown."

He laughs, almost as if what he just said were a joke, a hysterical ironic comment that should give both of us a chuckle. There is no real happiness or joviality there though, just a person reaching out. I stay focused and continue the interview. This isn't my first time.

"Could you please tell me if you experience persistent and unwanted memories, painful emotions associated with events, flashbacks, or repeated distressing dreams or nightmares, Sergeant Miller?" Of course, he has, I thought to myself—they all have who come to see me.

"Yes, to all of it. I went to Iraq; my f'ing job was disbursement—you know, just paying people. I thought I would be sitting in some makeshift hut disbursing checks. But that's not what I did. I f'ing went on every convoy across Iraq, up and down the f'ing death road over and over, and do you know what I did? You want to know what I did?" The veins in his forehead bulge as he continues. "I had to jump on convoys all the time with people who didn't give a shit about me; I had to carry millions of f'ing dollars, not little amounts, but *millions* of f'ing dollars with people who didn't know me, who I wasn't attached to and who couldn't give a f——k if I lived or died, because they didn't trust me. I would just jump on a convoy and ride around that f'ing triangle; we call it the Triangle of Death." His hands appear sweaty, and his face is contorted as he speaks.

Still listening to him, I turn and pull down a photocopied map of Iraq hanging on the wall. "Here, show me on this map," I tell him. "What do you mean you carried millions of dollars in money? Where do you call the Triangle?"

He marks cities on the map—Tikrit, Fallujah,

Mosul—and indeed, as the sergeant's shaky hand drags the highlighter across the page, a distorted triangle emerges.

He starts rambling, his hands shaking and his eyes darting around the room again, not quite resting on a single spot for more than a few seconds. "They knew the routes, the triangle."

"I still jump if I see a car coming down a road in my direction or see people up ahead near a road, and God forbid that they are bending over the ground next to a road." He is sweating now and clearly agitated.

"No one knew me; no one looked out for me there. We are supposed to never leave another marine behind, and I was really scared carrying that much money with no one knowing. I was riding with millions of f'ing dollars in cash, and as soon as we were blown up, I was left for f'ing dead. I wasn't on the manifest of the convoy; they went out to collect bodies and turned over those blown-up vehicles and found me under that burned-out Humvee, there with the money. I am sure if they knew what I had in my dirty little bag, they would have off'd me and kept the money— that's how much they cared about me. My shoulder still hurts, and I still wake up every night thinking about that, and I still have that bag. I used to think if I lost it, I would die. I still think I have to keep it with me."

"Do you have it with you now?" I ask.

He pulls out a small grimy but empty bag from one of the pockets in his pants. It has been folded multiple times and looks ragged and burned.

"I see, it looks like it has been through hell," I say. "So, I must ask you why you carried so much money, Sergeant Miller. You don't seem like you're delusional; it appears that what you say could be true."

He doesn't reply, as though he hadn't heard the

question, so I ask him again.

"Why carry so much money?"

He hesitates and then answers with a stammer, "You see on the news those accidents that happen when things are blown up in villages, things destroyed, and civilians are killed? How do you think the military handles it? We pay them off, and that is what my job was, and nobody in the military wants people to know. They are so f'ing concerned that I will tell someone their dirty little secrets that they are trying to get me certified as crazy … I think that's why I am here."

"So, are you crazy, Sergeant Miller?" I look him right in the eye and ask him again. "*Are* you crazy, Sergeant Miller?"

He doesn't blink. He looks me directly in the eyes and speaks with clarity and conviction, "No, hell no, but I am really feeling messed up. I have headaches, chest pain, but the MD says nothing is wrong with me medically. I have difficulty concentrating, trouble sleeping. I see other people are really trying to get me, get me out; they are done with me now that I am back, of no use, and they just want me gone."

I look down at his hand. It's quivering. "I understand the part of your anxiety and suspicion relative to your job situation, but are there any other factors as to why now, why today you are here?"

He pauses and sighs deeply.

"I just found out my wife has been cheating on me. She did once before when I was deployed, and we survived that, but now I just can't take it. I am so pissed, and I can't divorce her cause I have two kids and no judge is going to let a marine with my background have the kids. I am stuck; I can't sleep, and the last doctor we went to said she is bipolar, and if I can't take the ups and downs to just get out. I need help. I have nowhere to go with these feelings. I have taken Ambient to sleep, but I just eat that like candy. It does no good, and Trazadone leaves me feeling completely logy in the morning. It only makes things worse. I don't know what to do."

I put down my chart and ask him quite pointedly, "So do you feel you are fit for duty, Sergeant Miller?"

"Ma'am, yes, ma'am, I am fit for duty. I don't see things or hear voices. I have seen the guys who do, and they can't hide it, whatever it is that drives people to do things I would never do."

He puts his head in his hands and starts to cry. "I just want my life back, my wife and kids back to where things were better."

I get up and pick up a CD player with headphones. I pop in a soothing CD.

"Put these headphones on, Sergeant Miller," I say in a calm but clear voice. "This is bilateral soothing; it's part of what we call EMDR: eye movement desensitization and reprocessing. You will hear the sounds move from ear to ear, back and forth; it should help; it should soothe you. Just sit back and relax; don't think; there are no more questions for now; you are safe here. I want you to just close your eyes; I will turn down the lights. I am going to have you put these small discs one under each thigh, and you will notice a slight buzz alternate back and forth in sync with the headphones. Again, if you get a thought, just acknowledge it and let it pass through your mind, almost as if it comes in one ear and out the other. Focus on your breathing; slow it down. This will calm you and begin the process of getting yourself back—getting your mind, body, even your soul, back ..." I trail off as the sergeant closes his eyes and focuses on his breathing.

The room glows with a soft light, illuminated only by the one window facing westward, as the sun is still rising in the east. It isn't warm or cold, but comfortable, and this will help with the sergeant's relaxation, I think. The small lamp in the corner gives off an artificial orange glow, creating an eerie feeling of sickness in combination with the green and yellow carpeting. The scene would seem unhealthy to an onlooker, but to me the day has started normally.

"I am going to let you relax for now. I will be back in ten minutes, and we can work on stress reduction," I say with assurance. He nods in affirmation. Somewhat comfortable now, he kicks back and puts his feet up on a chair, headphones in place and pulsing discs under his thighs. His breathing noticeably deepens, and his face relaxes. This part of the EMDR therapy appears to be working, as he becomes visibly less stressed.

I open the door, sending one of the guards leaning against it onto the floor.

"Lance corporal, please don't disturb him. You can stay here, but please don't open the door. Thanks," I say curtly.

I make my way to a separate unoccupied open office. I pick up the phone, and with the chart that accompanied the sergeant, I read a number and punch in the appropriate digits.

"Is this Commander Watkins?" I ask.

"Hello, Dr. Fox, what do you have for me? Is this guy fit or however you want to say it? Can we trust him not to lose it?" The voice is eager. Obviously, he is concerned about this kid—or at least about whatever missions or task he needs done.

"He is in pain, sir," I respond. "I will need to see

him again. Do you know his wife or have any information regarding their relationship?"

By asking the commander this question I focus on treatment and not the covert concerns. I will get to see him again if I concentrate on the marital issues, and he may have a chance to get some help before he is deemed disposable and separated from service. The commander responds after a moment of hesitation, "Negative, ma'am. They came from Camp Lejeune, and he has been deployed several times from that base. He just came here from Iraq, found out about her infidelity, and started crying in the disburser's office."

I look at the notes, and then out the door at the guards.

"Sir, why are there guards with this service member? His military occupational service (MOS) says he is a disbursement clerk. Theoretically he just cuts checks, makes sure they get to the right people, and the most drama he experiences is with someone angry that their check is short. Why is his mental fitness so important?" There is silence at the other end of the line. "Are you there, Commander?"

"Let's just say we need discretion here. Has he told you anything classified? Anything I need to know?"

This is the moment that is always potentially awkward with Command, but I don't hesitate. If there is to be any rapport with this service member before he is whisked away out of my ability to help, I must be firm and clear, but without psychobabble. Command hates psychobabble.

"Sir, he's just really upset. He seems to be able to do his job. He's very concerned about his relationship with his wife and family, and there is such a stigma about coming here, especially escorted, that it takes a while for someone to get comfortable. I would like to see him a few more times, with your permission; I think he would be open to it. I have him using some sound and bilateral EMDR soothing to relieve the anxiety; I don't think he is seeking medication."

"Very well, you have him for now. You just let me know if anything pops up—security issues, you understand. He is my marine."

"I understand completely, sir. I appreciate the referral, and I will do my best with this service member. Sir, if I have him agree to a schedule, could we lose the guards?"

"Not yet, Fox. I am still not sure about the risk factors; you will have to wait on that one. Remember, this is my marine."

I change the subject with Command. I know that the line of communication is closing fast, and the only way to be productive with Command was to move onward—always forward.

"Sir, do you still want me to speak with the female engagement team (FET)? Isn't the first Lioness group leaving in two months for Afghanistan?"

He yawns and answers slowly, "Oh, yeah, I forgot about that. I do want you to meet with them, and I want the chaplain to meet with them, too. I want you to talk to them about maintaining their cool, holding their emotions in check. I know they're women, but they are really on the front line now. "

"I understand, sir. Let me know when and where you need me, and I will be there." I hang up the phone and walk back down the hall. The two guards leaning against the door look anxious to leave. As I reach for the door handle, they both move to get up, and I go back into the dully lit room that is my professional life.

The sergeant, still kicked back and listening, opens his eyes. His once sullen face is relaxed now, and he seems calm. His breathing, slow and steady, is in much better condition than before, and he is no longer fidgeting with his arms or legs. He looks up and smiles. I sit down near to him and speak quietly.

"I am going to lend you this CD player and headphones with this CD," I tell him. "I want you to use it when you get up, at chow, and at bedtime. It should help you sleep. I am not going to refer you back to the hospital for now. However, if you feel worse, have your keepers take you to the ER right away. Give me a call or have your Command call when you are ready to see me again. Does that sound like a plan? Also, I need to confirm with you one more time before you leave, Sergeant Miller—do you have any suicidal or homicidal thoughts?"

"No, ma'am; I *am* angry; I *am* really upset, but I don't want to hurt myself." He responds quickly in an earnest voice.

"Very well then, Sergeant Miller, when next we meet, we will address your anger, your marriage, and your stability amid your life dissolving around you. I have not written down anything else, and I suggest you keep all matters related to disbursements in theater to yourself. Do you understand that such muttering to anyone could put you in jeopardy?"

He nods. "There is one more thing, Doc," he mumbles. "There are some people, like my wife and a few others, who think I kept some of the money and brought it back with me. There was a mortar attack at my last money drop; everything was destroyed, and Command just can't figure out if I dropped the money before or after the explosion. Man, there was nothing left. The f'ing place was lit up like a f'ing scene in *Tropic Thunder*, where the explosions are all happening, but nothing is being put down on film. It was like that, a big f'ing movie."

"Sergeant Miller, that's a very interesting addition to what you've shared with me today. That could get you in a lot of trouble. Is it true? Do you have any of the money?"

I must ask. I could say it was reality testing or something clinical, but I am fascinated by this guy's story, and now that he is more relaxed, he is letting his guard down.

"No, I really don't have any money, but my wife, when I e-mailed her from Iraq and told her, she said maybe we could work things out; maybe there would be a chance for us. That is everything to me, Doc."

"Well, right now you need to get some rest, calm down, get some good sleep, and get better, Miller. I would just focus on that and keep any stories to yourself. I have seen people doing whatever they could to keep their marriages together during deployment, especially when they're trying to deal with cheating, but this is a new one for me. Use the CD; go back to your Command, and call me when you can come back in."

"Thanks, Doc. I do feel better. Do I have to have those gorillas with me?" He gestures toward the waiting escorts.

"Yes. I did ask about that, and for now they're your best friends. When it's time to come here again, we'll work on that."

He gets up slowly, with headphones, CD, and player in hand. He begins to walk out, and then suddenly turns and lurches awkwardly toward me. I jump as he grabs me in a hug.

"Thanks, ma'am. It's been so hard, and I don't want

to say this, but I just don't know anyone I can trust or anyone who really cares. You're a good person; I can tell. You remind me of my aunt Glenda back in Texas."

"Miller, you have to believe that it's possible to get better. You must believe it yourself, or there isn't anything, any magic I can do that will change that. It starts with you." If he didn't believe it himself, then there would be no hope for him. There are enough people out there who don't expect these guys to come back messed up, and even more who think once they are damaged goods, they aren't worth keeping around.

He hangs on to me like a desperate child being pulled away from his parent; I take his arms from around my back and squeeze his hands with an affirmative motion. I open the door; the guards stand at the ready. They give him a dirty look as they all walk off together. I follow them outside and watch them get in the government-licensed car. As I turn around, I look at the sun still low in the sky. It is so early, but I feel like I have already worked a full day. I think I have done some good, and perhaps this is not the day it will all go south; the day I finally get pushed over the edge and quit this place. However, the FET group is next, followed by the domestic violence offender group, and my feelings could change.

Female engagement teams are also called the Lionesses. They are women engaging other women in the Afghani war zones. The female service members are sent into villages to speak with the women and get intel. They must always ask permission of the village men before they are allowed to set foot near a female and her family. Battle as we know it has changed completely in wartime. We hear about improvised explosive devices, people know that convoys are blown up and that army soldiers, marines, and Special Operations forces are injured in ways other than simply marching on the enemy in organized maneuvers. These females are on the front lines. Under the guises of school building for girls, teaching sewing to mothers, and offering nutrition classes for families, these Lionesses serve a deadly mission.

There are no rules of engagement anymore, no agreed-upon battle formations that the enemy follows. Afghanistan and Iraq are guerilla shit storms where decorated allied Afghani forces can turn on us and kill Americans. Urban battlegrounds can be places where people are hidden, enemies are alerted, and police allies are slaughtered for assisting American troops. Children carry hidden bombs and explode themselves on horrified American military fathers. Snipers are everywhere.

Female engagement teams make a difference. They are the only ones who gain access to women and children where they live, and they are the only ones who are permitted to search females at checkpoints where so much warfare takes place.

So how do I help prepare these women to do a task that no one else can do in these villages that are fraught with danger and betrayal? I talk to them as they train so hard. I give them a safe place to vent, cry (don't tell anyone), and rage against those that have betrayed them in the past or the female leader who treated them so badly within their own team.

I started facilitating the Lionesses with a support group. There had been rumors of sexual harassment by female noncommissioned officers leading the female engagement team as they trained and ramped up to go. No charges were filed, but I was brought in to build unity within the group and offer a place to vent. If further abuse emerged, I would be obligated to report it. As it turned out, the accused abuser was pulled from the deployment, and that helped a great deal.

I facilitate the FET group weekly, and at these sessions I always appreciate that it smells better in a room full of women. Male marine groups leave lingering odors that are distinctly masculine and burn my nose. It smells quite different when the FET group meets. Don't get me wrong, they are tough, sometimes so tough that they curse when it doesn't even make sense to curse, and they sweat just as much as men on summer days. But after they leave, staff members remark that there is always a mixture of finer soap smells and the scented hairsprays that keep their requisite lacquered buns in place.

I feel a special kinship with this group who dare to occupy a hostile foreign land—a kinship because of the mission they take head on of helping people who often don't want help. However, the danger they face, the battle they face, is something that is beyond my sensibilities. I only know the outcome when they return and are changed forever. They have seen atrocities that I can only imagine, that remain burned in my brain after the stories are told to me. They convey these stories with narrowed, glazed eyes and checked-out stares. The women typically lose about twenty pounds on the Afghani deployment. They don't eat well over there, and they are constantly on the move. They often have stomach discomfort from being polite to villagers by eating foods that make their digestive tracks convulse. What they do really matters.

Today only Molly arrives. She says that the others are in the gas chamber with their masks on, training for whatever could come their way. She tells me that she imagines that right about now their eyes are burning and tearing, but she's sure that each one will make it through. "It's important to embrace your gas mask when you're out there," she says, "because you never know what'll happen next, and you have to anticipate the worst."

Molly has a strong and sturdy build. Her breathing is deep and slow when she speaks, which gives a breathy quality to her diction. She is unusually poised for an enlisted female marine and holds herself with erect posture and neatly trimmed nails. She is a voracious reader of Russian fiction, and she keeps a lock of her grandmother's hair in a gold locket she wears around her neck. She says it keeps her strong. Her grandmother is her hero, but she holds the reasons why close to her chest.

I enjoy working with Molly. We have known each other for three years. We met when she returned from her first deployment, and we met up again when she finished her second tour. She is originally from Iran and came with her parents to America when she was three; she is fluent in three languages spoken in Afghanistan. She is tall, quiet, twenty-three years old, and single. Molly is not her given name; she thought it best to Americanize it to fit in.

"Since it's going to be just you and me today," I say, pulling up a chair, "why don't we sit down and talk. Maybe you can tell me more about the work you do so I can help the group better."

She takes a deep breath. "We just don't know who the enemy is, and where females are concerned, the battleground is really heating up. The security checkpoints are one of the most formidable battlegrounds, and we female marines want in on it. We have been kept out too long, and now we have a chance to really be in the action in a major way.

"It's true that a checkpoint usually is the last point of return for a suicide bomber or a fuel- and bomb-laden truck on its trajectory to blow up barracks and personnel. And at checkpoints female Afghanis pose some of the greatest threats. No man can touch a female in the Afghanistan culture, so the FET marines make the difference. We do really important work."

Molly trembles with resolve when she speaks. "Make no mistake, every time an American female marine approaches an Afghanistan female, the marine is in extreme danger. These bad guys are putting on burkas and blowing us up when they're dressed as women. We can't touch those "women"—you know what I mean— and the military can't get anywhere near to search them as men. Female marines must do that job.

"We are tasked to go into the villages, talk to the women, gather intel, and get the hell out without getting blown up, shot, or abducted and worse."

Molly is strong and firm when she speaks. "Warfare has changed completely, and women are now on every battleground whether the media showcases it or not. We're suffering the same injuries as men but aren't getting the same pay and job designations. I know lots of women marines who come back the same way as men with combat stress, concussion, brain injuries ..."

Molly's upcoming deployment will be her third. Most FET members only go once. The Marine Corps doesn't usually send women into the villages with the team multiple times but if they know the languages, their services become more valuable. The word is that the Marine Corps wants others to get a chance, but rumors tell a different story of combat stress, anger, and disillusionment.

Molly has a unique perspective. "The truth is that the Taliban is still a formidable influence and women will never be treated well under their influence, including getting a real education, rights even close to men, and self-determination. It just ain't gonna happen."

I thank Molly and ask if there is anything else she wants to get off her chest, and she shakes her head no. I ask whether she is okay to go now. I always ask that before the group members leave. It is important not to let someone mask themselves in silence within the group and explode later.

I tell Molly to give the team my best and I will see them next week.

Chapter Five

———◆———

Intimate Partner Violence Screams

Domestic violence at Camp Pendleton is growing rampant. In the civilian world, offender groups are fifty-two weeks long. The experts, statisticians, program managers, and the rehabilitated all agree it takes at least that long to effect change in an offender. Marine offender groups are sixteen weeks max. There is little time for offender rehabilitation when the main job is to kill the enemy. The first four to six weeks are focused on accountability for violent actions. The next twelve weeks are designed to build communication skills, real-time intervention in relationships, and ongoing group support. However, the mission must come first, and the mission is to kill. So, deployments often break up these weeks, and killing people during treatment may not actually aid in maintaining nonviolent relationships when marines return from combat. I suppose it's rather like a junky going through rehab and getting a hit every quarter of the way through.

The first phase of treatment assists an offender in breaking through their denial—minimizing the offense and blaming the victim. As the offenders come from up and down the chain of command, there are varying degrees of compliance and self-revelation. Officers are seldom seen in the DV groups, and when they are it is because they are at odds with the Command.

The Camp Pendleton marine domestic violence treatment groups meet in stark conference rooms and classrooms in the counseling services building. The rooms contain drab military furniture. Wooden chairs surround large tables, and American flags stand by every door. Each room is painted a pale yellow. The windows are covered with a film of dirt that has been there since before President Bush stopped by. Marine motivational posters adorn the walls.

A clock sounds off 0800; through my window I can see a group of uniformed men step out into traffic and stop all oncoming cars for "colors." With their rifles shouldered, they move with authority and halt directly in front of the vehicles. A band begins to play. I remember when I first began military service, I thought there was an actual band playing every morning. I used to strain to see where the band was marching or sitting to play. I know now it is a recording, but it is played with such volume and fidelity that I can feel the notes on my skin, and I am still sure the band will step around the corner any minute. It can be heard for quite some distance, playing the "Star-Spangled Banner" and then segueing into "Waltzing Matilda" out of respect for the Australians, who offered aid to the Marine Corps during WWII. Several uniformed individuals wearing formal uniforms called Charlies, camouflage outfits called cammies, or full-dress whites, which are the navy uniforms, stop and salute. They look so young.

As a woman in my forties, I am old by their standards.

Most of these warrior kids are as young as eighteen to twenty-two. This can make even the most optimistic, assertive, and direct older person feel a bit vulnerable at times. It's a good thing I have that doctor title. That's good for keeping them at bay most of the time and keeping me in the communication loop with some modicum of respect from them. That is, except for the narcissistic domestic violence offenders. These fellas view women in rigid roles and give them low importance in the chain of ... well, in any chain of decision making or leadership.

As I walk into the room with a bundle of files under my arm, a group member, a medical corpsman, approaches. He is twenty-two, a petty officer second class. He is affable enough, but his file reveals something quite different—a young man who has seen violence growing up, is desperate for recognition in his medical career, and can't come to grips with his own domestic violence. This last seems in marked contrast to his dedication as a healer in medical service. He is at once caring and concerned and then controlling and domineering with family.

He is followed into the room by Smith, a pale, emaciated marine dressed in cammies, always twitching, scratching, looking around. At twenty-four he is old for a PFC; he has lost rank twice. A Texan with charm, he has plenty of stories and constantly seeks medication, counseling, and attention for numerous injuries related to combat.

As usual, he rushes up. "Doc, Doc, can I just talk to you for one minute? I really need to talk to you."

I am annoyed. "Smith, I can't talk right now, I have group. Come back at 1500."

"But, Doc, I had another flashback, I remembered more about the bus and children and ..."

I had to cut him off. "Smith, just write it down; bring it in. We'll use it with the next session."

Smith persists, "Please, just a moment. Come here."

I step outside the door with him. I'm getting frustrated. "Smith, did you listen to the relaxation CD? Did you do the bilateral brain stimulation-butterfly hugs?" I cross my arms and tap my shoulders emulating a butterfly's wings flapping.

Smith is almost frantic. "Doc, I can't take it. I go to bed, I'm there, the lead gunner, I'm waiting in the dark, our rear Humvee is broken down, I'm sitting, shaking, in the dark, we see the bus coming, lights coming right down the road at us, we give them the first signal to stop, flashing the light to turn on their inside cabin lights, but they still don't stop. I shoot in the air—nothing, still coming. The lieutenant ordered me to shoot into the bus grill. Man, I was ordered to do that. I mean, I see it every night—boarding that bus, seeing those dead children, hearing those pissed-off people yelling at me, hating me, spitting at me. I can't take it!" Smith's head is perspiring now, and his speech is moving at a staccato pace.

He continues emphatically, "I need something; my nerves are shot, and I need something to help me, Doc."

I stop him. "Smith, you know I can't prescribe. I am a PhD, not an MD; that's why I sent you to deployment health. They can prescribe something for sleep or anxiety for you. Go back over there and come back and see me later. You made progress last time; the counseling seems to have really helped. I have to go."

Smith looks defeated. He stops talking, begging for drugs. "Okay. But I really don't like them at deployment health. I wanna stay with you. Man, I hate those docs ..." Smith's words trail off as he leaves. I put down the files at the head of the conference table. The corpsman remains standing at the edge of the room. Then he moves toward me.

"I think I know that guy," he states with assurance. "Do you know what his MOS is?"

I feel distracted by getting ready for the group, so I brush him off.

"He must be a grunt, isn't he?" I ask him, still not focusing entirely on the young man but more on preparing for the upcoming group session. "I didn't look at his Command. He's gone through a lot. Maybe you treated him in Iraq or here at the base medical?"

The corpsman is not satisfied. "I don't know. Something doesn't feel right about that guy. My gut is telling me something. I trust my gut."

I turn to the other service members entering the room, "Come in and let's get started." They wander in, and I immediately recognize the faces of those I have treated before. They stand out to me every week as if they are the only ones in that moment that matter; yet every week we lose some and gain some. The cycle continues. Some will come back; others will die. They all start by hating to be here.

Martinez is twenty-one, the only woman in the offender group. This is highly unusual; a woman would ordinarily not be in a men's group. But we serve Command, and they would only allow her to participate on that day and at that time. So, she is here. She is more victim than offender and continues to blame herself for the DV perpetrated upon her. Her file has multiple incidents of domestic violence, which she as a victim endured for years with her husband. But because of a random act while protecting herself, she was volun*told* to come to an offender group. Most group members have witnessed domestic violence growing up, and she is no exception. She has suffered a lifetime of abuse from her family— physical abuse from her mom and emotional abuse from her father, who always kept a mistress. Her mother stayed in the loveless marriage and set an example of dependency, fear, and lack of self-confidence. Martinez has been married three years and has a very young child. She doesn't understand the depth of depravity of her service member husband, but she is protective of her daughter Angel. A beautiful Latina woman who just made corporal, she stays in a violent relationship (she says) for cultural and religious reasons. She is her mother's daughter.

Group member Jefferson Booth swaggers in, a lance corporal who speaks with a deep Georgia drawl. He is tanned and handsome, with huge muscled arms and a no-nonsense manner. Booth grew up in the South in a small town where abuse was just the way things were done. Alcoholism, physical violence including domestic violence, child abuse, and verbal abuse were just the way people lived. He is no longer with his spouse. He is an alcoholic like his dad and is really trying to end the legacy of abuse that runs in his family. He appears to have emotional insight but under pressure relies on threats, physical violence, and hurting pets to get back at his spouse.

Lamar Tatum is the next to arrive. He has post-traumatic stress disorder to the max, and he is a proud African American man who has seen too many deployments. He still carries episodes of war in his head. He can't smell or eat barbecue—the smoke from burning flesh—without setting off emotional grenades in his head, causing him such pain that it leaks out, contaminating his family and Marine Corps relationships. He often cries out that he feels like he is in quicksand, dissolving into tears and fits of rage he can't control. Tatum is twenty-six, the oldest in the group, but he can't seem to make sergeant. They have him managing the barracks now, so if he hears the distant memories outside the wire, he can't get into too much trouble. He will see no more real deployments, just the ones in his head.

Tatum speaks up. "Hey, did you start before me? That's not fair; I want to talk today. Last time you hogged the whole session, corpsman."

"Wait!" I direct. "We have someone new coming in, and the others aren't here yet. Remember what we said about personal responsibility; that's what we work on every day. We are responsible for where we are right now, who we are with, and what mess we have gotten ourselves into, no one else. We are living the dream, gentlemen."

Tatum reacts, "That's easy for you to say, Doc. You don't got no issues; you got that doctorate, a good job, great family—I heard you talking about your kids. What do you know about pain?"

I roll my eyes dramatically on purpose, and everyone breaks out into laughter. Humor is important in these groups. The tales are so dramatic and the pain so palpable that humor is a release. There is often nervous laughter, too, that comes when one faces one's demons. I wait a bit. "Oh, you don't think I know from experience, Tatum? You're right about me not having your same experience, but I have my own, my own pain, I can assure you. No one gets out of this life unscathed. I must keep my boundaries secure when I'm around you, so I'm not going to get into my personal business with you, but I can tell you I know about pain, and I know partners do things as well. We have you work on yourself in here because really that is all you have control over. If you come back week after week and stay stuck in a violent relationship, whose fault is it? It's yours, short and sweet. It's about you and your decisions that create your life. Just like me, I come back here week after week and hear the pain, see the bruises, and if I don't feel like I am effective or if I start taking it home, then it's time for me to reevaluate."

The manager of the domestic violence counseling program walks past the door and pokes her head in. "Are you about to get started, Dr. Fox? Time's a-wasting! Are you wearing your name badge? Remember to use your first name with our service members; it establishes rapport. And you'd better get started."

Tatum bursts out in my defense, "She's doing a fine job. We're waiting for some other folks, ma'am."

The manager looks at her watch. "Very well, but I want this door shut in five minutes and the blinds need to be at one quarter open, not too much, you know."

She turns and leaves. Tatum is still upset by the interloper. "Ma'am, that would drive me crazy. I think it's bad at *my* shop! Does she pick at you all the time like that, Doc? I thought you being the doc and all nobody would treat you like that in your own house."

I smile; I appreciate his concern for me. So often in offender groups men have no empathy; they mimic concern to mask their narcissistic ways. But Tatum is genuine. I know that his ability to feel empathy could be the single key to ensure he doesn't come back to this group. Other members repeat the cycle and either come back to group or straight to the brig because the violence escalates. I respond warmly to him.

"Tatum, did you ever hear that old Bob Dylan song about everybody gots to serve someone?"

Tatum nods his head. I think he can feel my warmth

even if he has never really known a Bob Dylan song and didn't get the analogy. I continue, "Well, like I said, we are living the dream, and even if no one appreciates what you do, if there is no intervention to alleviate your stress, it's up to each of us to evaluate a situation and figure out what is best for our own needs, wants, and desires. We must keep the faith, Tatum, and if we are ethical with our responsibilities, like our kids and our job, it is our moral imperative to blaze our own trail. You get my drift?"

Tatum looks perplexed. "Are you talking about me or you, Doc?"

I slow down and realize what group I am addressing. "All I am saying, Tatum, is that power and control issues are everywhere. To be aware of your own is everything."

Two more men walk in and join the group. They look around and find seats.

Matt Carson, twenty-three, is a corporal from radio battalion, a spook, which is the term for a marine who operates undercover and accomplishes a wide spectrum of clandestine tasks. He arrives without a history of abusive behavior; he is a caretaker, sensitive and embarrassed by being put in an offender group. He was trying to keep his ex-wife from driving drunk when he tried just a little bit too hard and was arrested for domestic violence. He is of slight build, very smart, and the least threatening presence in the group.

Ray Goodman, twenty-one, is a skinhead. He looks haunted, depressed, and gaunt. He stares downward and is slow in his response. His life before the military is shady at best, and he never refers to it in group. He is a helicopter mechanic who has little insight, tries desperately to control his wife, and has lost contact with the young son he cherishes because of the trauma his son has experienced in witnessing Ray's domestic violence.

I wave them over to sit at the table with the rest of the group. Often new members try to sit in the back away from group interaction, but that is never acceptable, and I always direct new members to join the group. Whenever someone new comes into the group I go over the rules, expectations, and how they can get out of here. I try to make my presentation very formal to gain their respect.

"I am Doctor Fox, your group facilitator. You are here because someone at your Command sent you here in response to a recommendation from a military case review committee, based on police reports, Child Protective reports, or other motivators that got you here. In my world you are here voluntarily."

I am interrupted by a big snort and laughter from the incumbent group members.

I respond to the snorting. "In *your* world you are voluntold to be here."

Booth speaks out, posturing as a leader of the group. "There ain't no dipping, no smoking, no eating, texting, calling, or falling asleep."

I nod. "What I do is simple. I am here to help you be accountable for just what you did. I don't know all your stories, but it goes something like this. You see a cell phone photo, text, or hear a voicemail. Or you have a friend on Facebook who tells you your spouse is cheating or been seen talking to someone or posted a photo or there has been a relationship change that triggers you. In person you might have the same argument over and over, but the incident that got you here happened something like this."

Booth breaks in again. "You got a text, e-mail, letter, phone call, look, gesture, or something else and you got a 'hot thought ...'"

Booth raises his fingers in air quotes and continues,

"So you thought—or maybe it was for real—that you were being cheated on or were gonna be cheated on."

Tatum joins in. "You could feel betrayed, financially ruined, disrespected. Or something from the past came up, your daddy or mommy left so you were hurt, lost, abandoned, just f'ing ruined, none of which is 'conscious.'" He raises his air quote fingers.

I pick up the familiar refrain, "That happened in a flash of a moment, and you went down a path where your heart was pounding, your jaw was tightening, your fists clenching ... And you got right to extreme anger. Well, what we know is that anger is a secondary emotion and that underneath is fear, resentment, embarrassment, some other deeper feelings that are old, related to a childhood hurt or young adult emotional wound which, when it all gets cooking, explodes into an action that got you here. Are there any questions?"

The sound of silence in the room is profound and peculiar. Usually someone makes some sarcastic remark, but at this moment, everyone is staring with jaws dropped. Tatum is the first to speak up. He mumbles to the group, "But my situation *is* different. She was the one who started it; she tried to push my buttons; I know she did!"

The medical corpsman speaks up for the first time in group. "Doc, isn't Lamar Tatum DMBing?" He points his finger at Tatum, not aggressively, but even these little gestures need to be diffused so as not to lead down the wrong path.

Carson looks up and appears confused, "What's DMB?"

"All right, let's start here for the new group members," I continue. "DMBing is denying, minimizing. or blaming. You aren't going to be allowed to do any of those. Denying looks like 'I didn't do it; the police report is wrong; it never happened.' Minimizing is 'I just pushed her; I slapped her but didn't use my fist, it didn't really hurt her.' Blaming is—well, Tatum, you just told us, didn't you? 'She caused it, pushed my buttons; it was stress; it was the alcohol.' So, don't do the DMBs and you'll just glide through group. You are only responsible for the facts of what got you here."

Martinez, the petite Hispanic woman sitting at the table, speaks in a low tone, "There is one little thing more. You can't say what *she* did, at all. Like I can't say what *he* did."

I am prepared for this. "Yes, you are gonna really, really, really want to tell how she/he started it, that you were just trying to calm her down, help her some other way. But what got you here was the choking, the strangling, or slapping or pushing your spouse." I stood up and went to the center podium. "Have we covered everything? Oh, I'm sure there's more, but it's a lot to take in for today. Remember this is a very large base but a very small world. Don't share group member stories outside of group. You will hear stories worse than your own; don't share them, you want us to keep it confidential that you are here, so keep it that way."

Booth interrupts, "With all due respect, ma'am, there ain't nothin' confidential about coming here, and everybody in every shop knows when somebody comes here. We get so much shit for just coming here. We hear 'woman beater'—'pet killer,' in my case—and even if you just come here for counseling, people can mess you up over it. You guys know I'm right; the rumors around here fly."

He motions with his hand like a bird flying up and away. "I know this one guy who was sent here from the brig for counseling 'cause they thought he off'd his spouse; man, and he ended up being strangled in the f'ing brig while he was on suicide watch." He starts laughing, "The funniest part was he didn't even do it, man; people just thought he did and that was it!"

Booth grabs his throat and pretends to squeeze it, crossing his eyes.

The corpsman admonishes him. "Shut up, Booth, you don't know what the hell you're talking about, man; you and your f'ing downhome bullshit."

Booth chides him back, "OOH, looks like I upset the little medic man." He crosses his huge arms and puts his feet up on the desk.

In moments like this I must take back the group or it disintegrates into name-calling and the potential for physical violence. The line is thin.

"Booth, put your feet down, and let's get back to business; you two are going to be in here longer if you don't focus on the group, not on the fantastical world outside."

Everyone laughs.

Tatum tries to help get the group back on track. "Aren't you going to tell them about check-in? That's the worst part; why don't you tell 'em. You have to say what you did over and over and over again, every week, like a friggin' AA meeting or something. 'My name is Lamar Tatum; my wife's name is Georgia; I have a son Caleb, who is three, a daughter Stella, one. My wife was pregnant at the time; CPS took the kids for a week; alcohol was involved, and the incident that got me here was …'"

I must stop him, "Wait, Tatum, it's not time for that, but I appreciate your enthusiasm."

Everyone laughs. The group shouts out in unison,

"Oorah!"

Out in the parking lot an SUV with spinner wheels and Texas plates sits with the motor idling. PFC Smith is sitting in the front seat looking around nervously. A young Hispanic teen in civilian clothes approaches the SUV on the passenger side. Smith unlocks the door and waves him into the car, reaches behind the seat, and hands him a package. The hooded unshaven teen starts to unwrap it.

"Are you crazy? Don't open that here. That's just enough to keep you covered; it's just the start. Now you just go to their house, get the good jewelry, the gold jewelry, nothing else; it should be easy. Just do that, and I'll meet you at my place. I'm gonna get Doc Fox to give me another referral, and I am gonna have more Vicodin by tonight."

The Hispanic speaks in accented English, "I thought you say she no MD, she can't do nothin' that can help with gettin' stuff."

Smith stops him cold and speaks with condescension, "No, she ain't no MD, but she's gonna help me and not even know it. She can tell 'em how really messed up I am; how I'm suffering ... that will do it. She can get it for me ... and you aren't going to get caught. The sergeant and his wife are at the game, and they won't be back until really late. Get in their house and get all the jewelry you can; if you see anything else we can sell just grab it. Now get the hell outta here."

Smith unlocks the door and the teen jumps out and heads back to his beat-up Honda civic parked across the street. He leans forward below the window view and snorts a white powder sprinkled on a map holder in his lap. He holds one side of his nose as he tips his head back and makes a snorting sound. He follows with the other nostril and wipes his nose. He looks around and catches the eye of the corpsman sitting in the group room staring out the window.

In the conference room, the group is still going on, and I see the corpsman is staring out the window. He has been watching the action outside in the SUV with Smith, the PFC who had been speaking to me. He clearly just saw him (and I did, too) snorting some white powder out in his ride—coke or H, who knows—and judging from the corpsman's expression, he doesn't like this guy.

Booth notices the corpsman staring out the window, "Medic, corpsman, hey! Are you with us here? You look like you're far away. We're talking about some important shit here."

Avoiding another argument, I continue the orientation. "Each week we have a lesson that supports you in establishing nonviolent relationships ..."

Carson blurts out, "I am never going to be in another relationship!" The group laughs again. This is definitely not the first time I have heard that declaration. It is important when someone new to the group makes such a statement to normalize the experience. "I know you mean that now, but people often come in here swearing never to be in another relationship or saying that they're in a new relationship with a totally different person since the incident that got them here. Stats show that in the future you will most likely be in another relationship. Trust me, gaining insights about what your own actions were that got you here and developing new communication skills can help the next time."

Martinez begins to speak again in a low and meek manner; she is interrupted by Booth's southern drawl, "Hell, Martinez, I want to understand where you're coming from, but Christ, you are a f'ing marine, strong, tough, and trained to master your rifle. Why the hell do you talk like that? Why don't you stand up for yourself? Are you this way fighting with your brothers? How the hell could they trust you ..."

I cut through his words, "Booth, stop! Let me tell you, even the most successful warriors and leaders, male and female, can be one way at work and totally submit, lose their power in abusive relationships. If we don't do something different, change our beliefs, we repeat the same patterns with our spouses over and over. We are what we were raised to be, the good and the bad. What we were exposed to, what we saw our parents or caregivers do, how they treated men and women, their parenting. We are a sum total of all of this, the good and the bad. I say that again because it's not what they told us to do, it's what we saw; what we heard; how we were touched."

Martinez speaks louder and with more purpose. "The other thing I've learned is that some of the people in our group have seen it growing up, I mean *seen* it— violence or abuse—I know I did. I think I am beginning to see how that has affected me, my relationships. I know my husband has justified what he did."

Carson's words are strained, "I thought you couldn't say what he did."

Martinez looks Carson directly in the eye and leans forward, putting her hand on his arm.

"You're right. I think seeing that stuff and some other experiences growing up have—what did you say, Doc Fox?—they shaped my beliefs so that under stress, I do think something justifies emotional abuse or physical force in power and control of a loved one. Something to think about, I guess. Has anybody else here seen your parents hurt each other physically or emotionally or been abused yourself as a child or teen?"

No one says anything.

I wait for comment from the group. "That's a first for this group—silence, no comment. Maybe that hit home."

The corpsman looks like he is drifting off again. I announce a break and take him to my office.

"What is going on with you, corpsman?"

"I'm sorry, ma'am, I just feel like I'm spacing out. I do remember some heavy shit in my life, and I just can't talk about it."

"I'm here now, corpsman, if you want to talk about it."

"It's so weird. It's like I can bring it up right now in my head, Dr. Fox, and I am back there, back with my dad, and I am here but I am there too, right now, in this moment. I am flashing back far away from here. I am this kid in a house in suburban Detroit. It used to look so big to me but my adult me sees it as a small bungalow with worn furniture and a funky old TV with antenna. Does that even make sense to you?"

"Sure it does. Talking about this stuff can take you back, but it's safe here to look at it."

"I am this small boy facing the TV, with the remote in my hand. That's so creepy; I am here, in this group with you because I threw the remote at my spouse and injured her. Is that ironic?"

"Go on."

"I see I am alone; there is a horrible smell of alcohol from a cheap whiskey bottle half full sitting next to the recliner with a burned-out cigarette sitting in an ashtray. I pick up the remote next to the whiskey. I managed to find my favorite show by clicking through the channels. I was proud of myself, seeing the time and finding the right channel. I just wanted my dad to see it. I wanted him to watch it with me. I loved that purple dinosaur, and I felt I was one of his friends. I started singing the song with them and went to get my dad.

"The big purple dinosaur was so real and I was so young. I can't believe how I can put myself right back there, all those years ago but I remember everything. I can see the sights, take in the smells, the effort it took to try and reach my dad.

"'Dad, Dad, just watch me, watch me, be with me and my friends, come in here, Dad.' I called to him in the bedroom. I see the shadow of this round guy in his forties, about five feet, eight inches tall, with another bottle in his hand. He comes around the corner stumbling, he sees me, but he doesn't love me.

"I am singing out with the characters on the TV, 'I love you, you love me.' 'I found the show, Dad! I did it myself, and I found the show!' I was so proud of myself. I think that was the last time I was proud of myself, except for when I was deployed. I had no idea of what was about to happen."

Corpsman breaks down crying; I reach out and put my hand on his arm for comfort. It seems like hours had passed since we entered my office, but this emotional heaving was taking minutes. I hear his stomach churning and see that his trusting, childlike naivety is destroyed. He appears fearful in the moment from something very long ago. I encourage him to continue.

"'See it, Dad, I know the whole song. I found it; I found the show!' My dad got closer, I could feel his anger oozing from him, leaking with the smell of alcohol. This was such a common feeling for me. I used to hide so often from Dad's anger, but I thought this time would be different. It wasn't, and I knew something bad was going to happen. I feel the same thing in group with some of these guys. I just froze, and Dad started yelling at me to give back the remote and turn off that stupid show." Corpsman was sobbing now.

"I couldn't move. I just felt frozen like the statues in freeze tag. I was so scared.

"'Don't hit me; please don't hit me.' All I know is that I see this huge hand grabbing for the remote, poking his stinking finger in my eye, and my eye burning. He was so damn drunk that asshole stuck his finger in my eye, and when he realized it, he wasn't concerned about me; he just wanted another drink and the remote.

"His big finger had gashed my nose. Blood was running down my face. No one was there to help me, to wipe the blood up or tell me they were sorry, and I just held it in. I can see that poor little boy just standing there like a soldier, taking it and being left there with the blood on his face and the dinosaur singing on TV.

"My dad just staggered back toward the bedroom

with the whiskey and the remote. I knew I would never treat anyone like that. I would treat my family better and offer help to anyone who needed it.

"My nose eventually stopped bleeding. I got my own supper and didn't see my dad until he slept it off, which took through the next afternoon." The memories are flooding now as he recalls his dad yelling horrible things about his deceased mother leaving him when he needed her most, leaving him to take care of a difficult and needy child, ranting about how hard he had it, feeling sorry for himself as always, especially as he fell into his drunken and violent rants. He recalls night after night his dad stumbling down the hall and back into his room to pass out.

"This time," corpsman says, "I just numbed out, wiped the blood off, went to school the next day and lied about how my eye got blackened. It was the beginning of trying to forget and deaden my pain. I realize now how much it has affected all my relationships.

"I swore I would never be like him, and I would always help anyone hurting. I realize that becoming a medic was my way of focusing on other people's pain and not my own."

He is noticeably disassociated; he looks checked out.

"Corpsman, are you okay?"

He snaps back as he hears my words.

"Yeah, I'm sorry; I'm ready to go back to group now, but I don't want to talk to the other guys about this yet, okay?"

Everyone is back from break when the corpsman and I enter the room. They are laughing.

"What's so funny?" I inquire.

Martinez tries to explain.

"I think the group is being really rude. Your boss came by, and when you were not in here with us, she said she was going to have to address that with you."

Booth snorts. "Ma'am, we just said you were her bitch, and we thought that was funny. Martinez didn't think that was funny."

"Who has kids here?" I ask. "What have your kids been exposed to? Corpsman just told me a story on break that has really stayed with him, and it was about what he saw and experienced as a child with an abusive parent. It's true for most everyone who comes through here that what we see as children can come roaring out in abusive behaviors when we are under stress."

Tatum raises his hand. Martinez also raises her hand.

Martinez speaks more boldly now. "I have a three-year-old daughter. She has seen way too much. Man, I don't know what she must think. She has seen her daddy throw me into a wall and pull my hair out."

I feel compelled to address the needs of a child exposed to such abuse. "You know they have child play therapy that can help. How do you deal with it when she acts out, do you use hitting or another way? Do you ever use time-out?"

Carson is fed up. "Hey, wait a minute. I just want to know how to get the hell out of here, how to graduate. There's check-in, but what about checking out?"

Group chimes in, "Oo-rah!"

I know that before any of them can address their demons they need to know what group success looks like, and how they can get out of the group. "Carson, take out the last homework assignment. What does it say?"

Carson removes the homework paper from his backpack and begins to read it. "I am totally responsible for the physical violence and emotional abuse I have done to my spouse/GF. She did nothing to provoke me or cause me to act the way I did. She does not have to forgive me; she may not forgive me, and she may remain afraid of me and not trust me."

I look at him and address him in a forthright manner. "Stop there. Can you say that today, Carson?"

He is visibly upset. "Hell, no. She's a marine; she started it. It was her, not me; she attacked me; she went crazy; she was drinking Jaeger bombs, man—I mean ma'am—she came at me, what am I supposed to do? If you come at me like a man, I gotta take you down, and we're told every day never let a marine drive drunk. She was gonna leave! This is just not fair!"

Booth, sitting back with legs out and arms folded across his chest, announces with a straight face, "My daddy says fair is where they judge pigs." Everyone just turns and stares at him for a moment.

I nod and put up my hand gently. "Okay, just stop. Carson, you have just made the point of why you are here, and until you can say that *why* yourself, you will still be here. This is just your first day; I know you don't want to be here. I know partners do things, but if you walk around letting other people control you by pushing those buttons, which are *your* buttons, you risk being out of control at any given moment. I know you control your temper every day."

Carson remains upset. "What are you talking about?"

"Service members come in here all the time saying that they know how to handle themselves, and they put the fault of why they are here, in a violent offender group, on the other person, their loved one, the love of their life. They start off saying that if someone gets up in their face they must do what they gotta do, right? You all are strong, trained, and know how to handle yourselves—'the few, the proud.' Right? That's tested every day in your profession as a warrior. I know you control yourself. You are challenged every day through physical and mental training not to lose your cool, to control your body, mind, and spirit. People can threaten you; insurgents can shoot at you; higher-ranked individuals can get all up in your face, screaming at you, telling you to do stuff you don't want to do, telling you stupid stuff that you know more about than they do, like officers who arrive in theater to lead you when they don't know jack."

Booth blurts out, "OO-rah!" Group starts looking at one another, nodding their heads—yeah.

"So, why can't you control yourself, your emotions, your physical violence with a loved one? Why can't you do that and stay proud, honorable, get the facts of an event, share your thoughts, feelings, or hurts with your loved one, your cherished one, the love of your life?" I stop speaking and let the words linger in the air. The silence sits there for a moment before I go on.

"Some people try intentionally to provoke you and do trigger your strongest emotions, your fear of being cheated on, betrayed, and lied to. I can tell you without knowing anyone's story here that this is probably what happened to you." I draw a timeline on the dry eraser board. "First you have this chemical or magical attraction; you can't wait to see each other, text each other, or just hook up." The room comes alive now; they are paying attention as I talk about hooking up. I look around the room as I move behind their chairs. Some have been doodling, some trying to text under the table. I reach under the table and startle the group by confiscating a member's phone. He objects but it is too late; I will give it back after group.

"Next"—I put another notch on the timeline—"you see something posted on Facebook or perhaps you see a photo or text or hear a voicemail when you break into her phone, and you automatically thought, maybe because of past experience, maybe not, that you were being cheated on. And then, you get further triggered and"—I put another notch on the line—"you call her that vulgar name, if she tries to leave you. You block the door, destroy a cell phone, grab her so she can't leave, so you can 'talk' or get to the bottom of it. Or maybe once you were triggered you just let her have it—strangled her, punched her, pulled her hair—because you wanted her to feel pain as bad as you did in the moment.

"So where is that *few and proud* noble intention then? Where are those *few and proud* values then? What you saw your parents do and what your beliefs are—'an eye for an eye' or 'women should …'—that justified your unleashing the dark side of the *few and proud* training that in that moment went terribly wrong. You had to silence your loved one completely to stay in control. Someone may have pushed those buttons, but they were *your* buttons, and it was you that lost control.

"As a warrior you must control your body and mind, and as a lover and intimate partner you must own your own reactions and emotions. That is why that graduation exercise would have you saying that your loved one did nothing to provoke you. You are responsible for your own actions, whatever you contribute to the relationship. Do you get that? Well, maybe not today, but maybe tomorrow or next week. That is the group's purpose, right there. Learning that could allow you to let love, safe love, into your life, and really empower you to embody the true value of being of the few and the proud that walk their talk and lead a life of honor, courage, and commitment.

"I think that's enough for today. Do the homework, participate, and you will get out of here. The homework this week is looking at what you contribute to the relationship. Don't focus on your partner; it's easy to blame her or him, or blame work, stress, alcohol. But when you strip that away, what is it you do and what can you change in you to get the love you want without minimizing what you did, denying your part, or blaming your loved one? See you next time; don't be late."

Group shouts, "oorah!" and files out. I pick up the records and take them to the file room to lock them up. I walk to the front of the office, looking through the glass window in the front of the building. It's beautiful outside, just the one SUV and the trees that line the building.

I turn to the secretary. "I don't have any other individual patients, so I'm leaving early. I'm going to go home; let the manager know. Tell the manager I will fill out a leave slip tomorrow." The secretary nods and I pick up my briefcase and leave.

Chapter Six

———◆———

NCIS Sam, a Loving Tone

I walk out to the car and activate my Bluetooth to call Sam and leave a voicemail. "Hey! I decided to finish group and go home. Give me a call when you get in town tonight. Sushi might sound good." I drive through the hills and up to my gated property. The gate pulls back, and I roll up the long tree-shaded driveway. A neighbor can be heard calling to me in the distance, and I wave at her as I pull into the garage building adjacent to the 1946 ranch-style brick structure.

I get out of the car and cross the flagstone steps toward the front door. I can smell the jasmine and orange blossoms. The rabbits are out feeding on the front lawn, much to my dismay. I wave my hands at them and they scamper away. I have remodeled extensively since I purchased this property, installing hundreds of feet of slate flooring throughout the house and busting down a few walls to expose panoramic views from each window. This gives me almost a 360-degree vista and adds to the calming quality of the property. I can come back from the most stressful day of therapy, and as I close the gate behind me, I can feel the stress dissolving. The views are of avocado groves below and on to Palomar Mountain, about thirty miles away. This is Fallbrook, a rural community that boasts avocados, citrus, and lots of flowers that dot the hills in the distance southward toward Bonsall. The racehorse farms can also be seen in the distance, landscaped with tall shady trees and white picket fences. My fifteen-year-old Springer Spaniel Rocko stands at the door just waiting to be let out. He used to chase after my old Porsche the entire length of the driveway and would pass me sometimes, but that was seven years ago and now his arthritis has slowed him down. He spends the days indoors now with Lola, my blue-eyed Siamese cat, cuddling together on the orthopedic dog beds placed throughout the house. This place is a constant project; the roof, walls, plumbing constantly need repair, but the love and warmth under this roof is palpable.

"Hey, you two, come here. Dog food plus turkey, and kitty food for you, Lola," I call to them from the kitchen.

The cat looks up with her blue eyes slightly crossed and meows. She jumps up to the table where her food is— it must be elevated or old Rocko, deaf and almost blind, will stumble upon it and eat it.

I put down the food and walk back down the hall to the bathroom off the master bedroom. I turn on the water in the bathtub and light a couple of candles. A portrait of my mother sits on the vanity ledge. She was a beauty, a 1940s Maureen O'Hara look-alike with thick hair, creamy white skin, and a smile to melt the hardest heart.

"Hi, Mom, another day done," I say with a sigh. "I am exhausted, fried, and well, you know … I miss you, Mom."

She has been dead for many years, and I can still

remember our conversations—the unconditional support and financial wisdom I would get when I became a single parent and just needed to sit on her couch, watching Lily run around, having some homemade soup and R&R. Mom's place was always good for that. She was a Missouri farm girl who could still grow anything, even in a Pasadena backyard. She used to boast that it was small, but she grew enough to feed the whole neighborhood. It just killed her when my dad went to Vietnam and didn't come back. No, he wasn't killed there, but he met another woman, a civilian employee, and never returned to us as a family. My mom became a single parent, went back to college, never married again, and I never remember her being sick. She was the epitome of stoicism—not necessarily a good thing.

She also never really wanted me to go into the psych field. She wanted me to become a teacher as she did, at forty-five with two kids to support. Even though my dad was a colonel in the army, he was not keen on providing for a family that he was no longer interested in. He has long since passed on as well. The irony of his death was that he was a John Wayne figure of a man, who led the fights on all fronts during WWII, came back unscathed from Korea and Vietnam, but was downed by a drunken trespasser on his ranch. My mother said he got what he deserved. It is so weird that I am the one who ended up working with the military.

Speaking to the picture, I wonder what Dad would have thought of my job with the military. "What you do think, beautiful lady? He never approved of much, did he? Broke your heart, and I guess he broke mine, too."

I close the bathroom door, so the cat won't join me. Two days ago, she came in while I was taking a bath, jumped on the tub ledge, and fell into the water, scratching me accidently as she flailed wildly to get out. I didn't need a repeat. I have a nice long soak, get out, put on my robe, and dry my hair. I pull out my LBD—little black dress—and my turquoise necklace and earrings and lay them on the bed. Picking up my phone to call Sam, I notice that he has left a voicemail while I was in the tub.

"Hello, Doc, I'm here. I've checked into the new officers' quarters. If a commercial hotel had a view like this, it would be hella expensive ... Yes, I did just say *hella* expensive. Man, I can't believe how much you guys at Camp Pendleton are building out here; you can really see it from the air. Call me when you're ready, and I'll meet you at the sushi bar, although the place we went last time was so loud that I would really like to go somewhere a little quieter, so we can talk. That guy who had his birthday at that last place must have almost had a concussion with that metal bowl on his head being banged by those crazed sushi chefs singing happy birthday. Anyway, call me."

I am almost ready, with the dog and cat staring at me in what I assume to be approval. I am looking pretty good for a forty-something gal, rocking this LBD; my hair is done, and my makeup is—well, it's okay. I pick up my phone and redial the message sender. I must leave a message as the phone goes straight to voicemail.

"I guess we're playing phone tag now, Sam. So, you want a different place, do you? Meet me at that Japanese restaurant closer to the beach on Pacific Coast Highway in twenty minutes." I walk down the hall to tell Blake where I will be.

"That's okay, Mom. I'm going out with Ronnie anyway. I'll be back by ten."

"All right. Love you!"

As I drive from the hills of Fallbrook to Pacific

Coast Highway I realize I am a bit nervous anticipating my meeting with Sam. He is an amazing guy who seems to be able to get through my most ardent defenses. I cruise pass the sushi bar where Sam didn't want to go. He was right—it already looks packed, and the sound of clanging pots and the YMCA song blare from the restaurant as I sit at the red light. I continue to the beach, with windows down and sunroof open. This is the best time to have an old sports car—twilight with the cool crisp air coming off the water. I still love the way this black car hugs the road and the contour of the seat fits my body. At times like this, the Porsche feels like a classic, not an old car without the restoration it needs. I pull into the parking lot of Hana Sushi, a quiet little place, family run, with diffused lighting and small intimate tables. There is a long sushi bar across from the door, but only one sushi chef, who barely notices me walking in.

I look around and see that Sam has already arrived. One of the things I like about this NCIS agent is that he is always fifteen minutes early and takes a booth in the back corner where it is dark. No one can come up from behind and catch him off guard. I walk over, and he stands up to give me a strong, warm embrace. I love, too, that he offers the strongest and most reassuring hugs. My smile must have lit up the room. He leans over, his six-foot frame bending to meet my five-foot height. He kisses me on the cheek and then whispers into my ear.

"It's so good to see you. I've missed you." I hug him back, and as I pull away I look directly into his eyes.

"You came all the way out here just to have a bit of sushi with me. I'm charmed!" I don't wait for a reply, but smile and take a seat next to him in the booth. He always sits on the outside, I recall. As soon as I sit down, the server comes over, bows, and brings each of us a small white sake cup with a single white ceramic carafe.

"I think I remembered your drink right—hot sake?" He points to the cups. He knows he got my drink right; he always does.

"That's right," I say. "But don't think you're going to get me inebriated—loose lips sink ships, you know."

Sam laughs. "Ha! I've *never* heard that before. Let's have a toast to you!"

He raises his sake in a toast and I reciprocate, "To you!"

It feels good to be with him as we drink the sake and both mark what we want to order on the sushi ordering sheet. The server retrieves it and leaves.

I thought I'd start with the obvious. "So why the fast trip out? You aren't on leave; there isn't a conference out here, and you aren't deploying, so why are you here?"

Sam appears uncomfortable. "Honestly, I was missing you and wanted to see you. I care about you and …" He trails off before reaching across the table to me. He leans over, takes my hand, and kisses it slowly.

I remain unconvinced. I know he is glad to see me, but he is here for a reason, an NCIS reason, so I persist, "And what? What is going on?"

Sam downs a gulp of sake. "I want to talk to you about your work."

"I see patients every day; I do those domestic violence offender groups, and I hold briefings. I've never heard you so interested in what I do," I say. "You know I can't tell you particulars about a case; everything is confidential except domestic violence, criminal activity, or substance abuse. There's nothing I've heard over this last week that meets that criteria, except maybe a drug deal I saw. Do you want to hear about that?"

He shakes his head. "Not now. I'm looking out for you; you just don't get it."

He downs another sake and motions for the server to bring two more. Sam is careful. He continues slowly, choosing his words carefully.

"I know who you see as clients, Sarah; monitors hear what you do, and your computer usage indicates wherever you go on the net. This new case you have with this guy and his little dirty bag could get you hurt, and I care about you."

"What?" I am really surprised by my reaction to what he is saying. My stomach tightens up, and I have mixed emotions. I care for this guy, but he is crossing a boundary. A boundary that has never been an issue before. I don't like it.

"Your intel guys aren't actually listening to my sessions, are they? You're getting to me quite a bit here; it's freaking me out a little." I don't know what to think exactly. Were all the counselors being listened in on? Watched?

Sam must be able to see the concern in my face. He asks, "Do you trust me? I mean really trust me?" His hand never leaves mine on the table. I can see he wants to stay close, and that he isn't trying to frighten me.

"Yes, I do. I mean, I'm getting to know you, and I feel comfortable with you. But it takes time to really trust, and what you just said crosses a line—professionally and personally."

I can see that Sam wants to get to the point fast before he loses me. The job is one thing, but he really cares for me, and I can see that too.

"I don't mean all that psychobabble stuff ..." I must look offended because he keeps on, "Work with me here. I don't mean any offense. I mean, if some kid who is supposed to just be admin at Al Assad tells you he has been all over Iraq during the most heinous incidents you've heard about on the news, and you start looking at where he has gone, how many times he has been blown up, and it really has nothing to do with his job, don't you wonder about that?"

"I haven't really thought about it. Hypothetically speaking of course, if there was such a kid who came in because he was in psychological pain, I would treat his pain, not examine his geography. Lots of these young guys come back from theater and may even exaggerate their travels, firefights, IED experiences, but it doesn't mean they're any less hurting. I don't try to find out if they're telling the truth about their job and where they've been. I saw this guy come in with a concussion, ringing in the ears, and PTSD. He made up this wild story about combat, and it turns out he was a communication guy, not a grunt, who was running to a radio tower in a sandstorm and fell into a pit. That was it, fell into a pit, and yet he was so injured, so upset emotionally but really didn't feel entitled to combat stress because his injuries were from something stupid like falling in a pit."

Sam is frustrated. "Why are you telling me this? You know I'm trying to look out for you. If you find out something classified or something that involved other people who were paid money to keep their mouths shut, you could become a target yourself, by the media or somebody else."

"Whoa! Just back off, Sam. I'm not sure what you know, but if you're listening to my sessions, that's a huge violation of the basic ethics of what I do." He really is in my territory now, and I'm angry. It's great to have someone feel protective, but not respecting my clinical expertise is another thing entirely. I decide to wait before offering any more information or hinting that he is right on in his knowledge of whom I have seen. He could be right, maybe. I could be in danger because of the questions I asked my patient. My gut was really churning now.

I change the subject to salvage the meal. "Really, Sam, let's just have dinner. I know you probably have an early brief tomorrow on things I really don't want to know about, so let's just enjoy the time together, okay?"

Sam starts to say something but is interrupted by the sushi arriving at our table. Instead of talking he divides the wasabi and ginger.

"How are Lily and Blake?"

I have chopsticks in my mouth, so I must wait to answer. I swallow the yellowtail with rice and dab my mouth with the napkin.

I am very relieved to move on. "They're great. Lily is at Pepperdine, and Blake is trying to decide where to go to college next year. He's in the top two percent of the country, so it looks like he has his choice, but his girlfriend goes to Cal Poly San Luis Obispo, so that definitely has the edge for now."

Sam swallows loudly. "You mean his girlfriend is already in college, Cal Poly?"

I raise and drop my shoulders. "Yes, I do. She's great—Nicole, a runner and equine science major. She and Blake have a very unusual relationship. They don't have a lot of drama. Lily has told him over and over not to choose a school based on a relationship, so we just got back from looking at Cal Poly for his engineering major, and I have to admit it was impressive on its own."

Sam is excited. "I love Cal Poly. I must get up to Vandenberg to observe rocket launches, and I've been there often. The wine country is up there too. Have you ever toured the vineyards?"

I am interested, and I feel more comfortable again. We're back to couple's conversation that feels safer and more familiar. "No, I've always wanted to do that, but I've just driven through the area. That would be a great thing to do."

Sam now is gazing into my eyes and speaking with a soft tone, a contrast to his rugged exterior. "I would really like to take you."

My stomach gets butterflies. In this moment I can honestly say such a thing is possible, even at my age and after so much time being alone and a single parent. Sam leans over and takes my hand. I am starting to perspire, and I blurt out, "Let's do it. I mean, that would be lovely, Sam; I would like to go to the wine country with you …"

Sam moves right past my "let's do it" faux pas. "Want to come see the new officers' hotel where I'm staying? Maybe get a night cap there? There's also a new lounge for the officers." We both know where that might lead, and as nice as that would be I have to be home before too long.

"No, I can't, unfortunately. I have to get back." I tell him Blake has a lab to do, I know, but I like to be home for him at least by ten or eleven. The server brings the check; Sam grabs it, and we stand to leave. He pulls me to him, and again hugs me and kisses the side of my head.

Sam seems to feel compelled to say one more thing regarding my patient. "Be careful, and don't write down anything that you wouldn't want reviewed."

I'm no longer offended; I've softened a bit. Maybe it's the sake or just feeling loved, but in this moment, I'm responsive to his concern. "I understand; I've been doing this for a while, you know." I smile and begin walking to my car.

I turn and tell him, "If you're going to be in town for a couple of days, come on over for dinner. Blake's never met you, and he's curious about this guy on the other coast that I talk about so much. I think you'd enjoy seeing our place. You can pick some avocados if it isn't too dark."

Sam brightens. "I'll call tomorrow; I'd love to come over and meet Blake, maybe pick some avocados, and I have to show you, guys with guns can still be farmers, ma'am."

I drive home smiling.

The next morning at counseling services I am back at it—another day, another offender group session. We sit in a circle in a room that's stuffy, with no access to the air conditioner.

Carson begins, "I had some trouble figuring out what you wanted on the homework, the MDB—what is that?"

Booth responds before I can answer, "It means you still won't cop to what you did, man. 'I just pushed her, I just yelled at her, I just, just, just, just ...' MDB, it means minimizing, denying, and blaming your partner. Denying is you didn't do it at all—'police report is wrong; she said later nothing happened.' Blaming is blaming her—'look at the wheel, she caused it, she was drunk, I was just trying to help her, calm her down,' or 'it was the alcohol, job stress.'"

I am impressed by Booth's words, "Awesome job, Booth; you get to leave early today, gold star."

Group shouts out, "Oo-rah!"

Martinez cries out, "But I think it *is* my fault."

Booth retorts, "Oh, hell no, you're gonna make us all stay later. That's why a chick shouldn't be in this group."

I have wanted to draw Martinez out, get her to process her feelings. "Say more, Martinez ..."

She's anxious, but tries to move forward, "The first time and the second time it *was* him. I had to recover in the hospital, and I almost lost my baby, Angel. He was put in the brig then and came to classes like this one, but this time I don't know, it happened so fast. We were at home and he ..."

Tatum interrupts her, "You can't say what he did; just what you did."

Martinez continues, "I know I need to talk about what I did, but I need help understanding, because I *do* think it must have been me who caused it. We were arguing over what I was wearing—shorts, they weren't even that short—but I saw his jaw clench and he started to make a fist and then let it go over and over. I got scared; I just ran to the nursery and locked the nursery door. I always feel safe in Angel's room—she was at my mom's. I heard the pounding on the door and I really thought he was going to kill me. I looked everywhere for something, anything to protect myself with and I picked up my daughter's little wooden horse. I was so scared; I really thought this was it, that he would kill me. I just picked up that small horse, and when the door broke off its hinges, I threw it. I didn't even look; I just threw it. The next thing I knew my husband was falling back with blood coming from his nose and forehead. I ran and got a towel, put him in the car. He was yelling, 'You hurt me, you hurt me, you bitch!' He couldn't believe I did it—stood up to him, I mean." All the men in group start laughing.

Booth is laughing the hardest. "Little pussy bitch. OO-rah!"

I am miffed. "Stop it. I don't know why when a woman tells what she did, the men always laugh. It's not funny. Anyone can be a victim."

Martinez goes on, "When we got to the hospital, he needed eight stitches, and I was arrested from the medical report identifying me as the offender. So, see, it *was* my fault."

Carson isn't buying it. "Man, that's self-defense, isn't it, Fox? They have this huge history of abuse, and this time he's breaking in a door to get to her, and she clocks him. If that isn't self-protection, I don't know what is."

I am concerned; this did sound a bit odd. "What did the judge advocate say at the case review committee?"

Martinez is articulate and ready with her response, as if she has recited it a thousand times: "They said I could have left when I saw him getting angry. They said I am a marine; I chose to stay, and I threw an object at him, which became a weapon, ma'am."

Booth turns on Carson, "Why you sticking up for her, Carson, you little bitch. You gotta be about calling her out on the MDBs, man."

Carson looks at Booth with a cold icy glare. "Don't you ever call me a little bitch again. You got that, you steroid-bulging hillbilly dick?"

I am right there. "Stop it, you two! This situation brings up a lot for everyone."

They continue debating what should or could have been done.

—◇◇◇◇◇—

The main NCIS office building at Camp Pendleton is new, completely new, and heavily laden with security fixtures and cameras that follow every move. If you are a visitor, or even if you are a DOD employee, when you enter, your laptop is taken from you, searched, and disabled. You are issued a badge, and your cell phone is also confiscated and returned upon your departure. The atmosphere is always at a heightened state of alert. Unmarked cars surround the building with antennas arrayed across both roof and trunk of each car. Inside the clandestine structure General Markham is sitting at a table with NCIS agent Sam Waters, Colonel William Hall, and Staff Sergeant Gilmore.

General Markham wants to get to the bottom of things, "So what the hell is this? Did this scoundrel, damn POG, excuse my language, did this guy take the cash? Is he trying to make his own deals? What in the hell is going on here? I need answers, gentlemen."

Colonel Hall, the area commander, is trying to get the information. "We still don't know, sir. We have interviewed his wife; she did have an extramarital affair while he was in Iraq and intended to leave him but said she was convinced by him that when he returned things would be different, that he had some big deal, something that would change everything and would make her want to stay with him."

General Markham has heard such stories before and is impatient. "That could be anything; service members lie all the time to spouses to just keep 'em to come home to. Waters, do you have anything?"

Sam remains calm—NCIS always must be calm. "The facts are these, sir. He did act as a disburser in highly classified situations; he did take large amounts of cash to places where collateral damage was assessed as best handled per payments. We are not sure how much he knew about how much he carried, but we know he was blown up at least once, found underneath a Humvee, and he does have continuous feelings of disenfranchisement because he was never attached to any one group, and he was actually left for dead, sir."

Agent Waters takes a breath and leans in. "We know he was hurt but completed some missions, disbursed capital, but whether he kept part of it, made separate deals, or just kept it all at any one time is a mystery."

He continues, "There was one time where there was a heavily engaged force at his point of disbursement and following the completion of his disbursement, that area was destroyed by a series of explosions. The individuals that were paid or intended to be paid were all killed, and the bombs destroyed everything."

General Markham remains impatient and unsatisfied by Sam's brief. "Can the wife give any more information?"

The general looks at the staff sergeant, who jumps in reaction and begins talking hurriedly: "I know this family. His wife is bipolar; she has ups and downs, and her Facebook page shows she is not into the marriage. They have two children, and I know the marine wants to try to save his marriage. Our company has arranged for him to get help at counseling services. He just keeps talking about his wife and her infidelity. I don't think it stopped when the marine got back. We have him doing jobs requiring no clearance and of no real importance until this mess gets sorted out."

General Markham gets an idea. "Who is he seeing at counseling services? Some of those therapists are flaky. I don't like the whole idea of spilling your guts—whoa, whoa, whoa—except, of course, for domestic violence. I have zero tolerance for that. My new policy is every marine engaged in a DV incident gets taken out of the home by PMO. No tolerance, I don't care whose fault it is. Someone's leaving that night, and everyone is gonna get treatment."

Everyone looks at one another and nods.

Sam speaks, "It's Fox, sir; Doctor Fox is the therapist treating Miller. She is very good. I have known her work for years; she is solid, respects the Marine Corps and serves Command. She will help but not get into areas that aren't related to the infidelity. I can vouch for her."

General Markham says, "We have to watch that little weasel. I have a gut feeling something ain't right here. We have a desperate marine, missing his wife, feeling cheated on and been in theater, blown up and doing shit he was never trained for—this is not good. It just don't feel right. But don't let anyone just administratively separate the poor bastard. Those battalions come back and try to cut out the screwed-up hangers-on, saying it's bad for morale to keep them around; we need tough and ready. We are not going to let this guy fall through the cracks; do I make myself clear, gentlemen?"

He gets up and walks out. The men follow and leave Major Waters and Staff Sergeant Gilmore behind.

Gilmore looks at Waters, "Man, I can't figure this out. I served with Miller. I would never have thought he could do something like the general is inferring. He was just some quiet guy, stayed to himself, simple job, and we used to make fun of him because he didn't party. He didn't break any rules; he just stayed to himself over there and e-mailed and called his wife. That's why they thought he would be good for jumping on convoys and going 'cause he wasn't attached to any group anyway. You don't think we contributed to him wigging out like that, do you, sir?"

Sam shakes his head, "I don't know, probably not. I

just wonder if there is anything here at all. He probably just did what he was supposed to, completed his mission and tried to tell his wife anything he could just to make her stay. Lots of guys do that."

The DV offender group is still arguing among themselves at counseling services. Carson defends Martinez to Booth.

"I think you're an idiot, Booth. No, I *know* you're an idiot; she isn't doing any of that. She's taking too much of the blame."

Booth puffs up his huge chest and flexes his massive biceps. "Screw you! You want to take it outside, man?"

Carson is strong with great resolve. "No, man. I've had enough of fighting. I don't want any more to do with fighting with anyone anywhere."

Corpsman says, "What are you talking about? Are you talking about not deploying anymore?"

"Yeah, I don't want to go back again. I did it; I think it changed me. No, I know it changed me forever, and not in a good way either. Don't get me wrong, I served for all the right reasons, and I'm proud of what I did, but I'm done with fighting. That's all I can say. I'm done, and I'll deal with my demons and move on, but I'm done."

Corpsman feels compelled to engage. "Not me; I need to go back. There I'm Doc; I'm the doctor who everyone respects, the person they go to. I can make decisions there, life-or-death decisions, and I'm respected, not some baby back bitch here that can't do shit without some young POG asshole that doesn't know dick about anything telling me what to do. I gotta go back; I feel alive there. I'll die here."

He looks up at me. "And, no, I am not suicidal, and, no, I am not homicidal, so you don't need to call anyone, and no one needs to watch me, okay?"

"So, corpsman, how do you really feel?" I quip.

Everyone laughs. Booth has been triggered. His adrenaline is pumping, and he can't calm himself down. "That is bullshit! Ain't nothin' alive there. Why don't you tell us about the swamps, wading through those f'ing swamps with those f'ing bugs and those hajjis chasing you down and shooting at you or those f'ing daisy chain bombs, those mother f'ing bastards ..."

I have to ask, "Why do you keep saying f'ing, Booth?"

He blushes and looks bashful, in sharp contrast to his previous rant.

"Sorry, ma'am. I was raised not to speak that way in front of a lady."

"Well, thank you. We ladies do appreciate your showing respect by watching your language. Let's stop here before we start accessing anymore flashbacks and have to do 'eye movement desensitization and reprocessing' just to get through the first part of group. Listening to you guys and gal, you'd think that you were the victims. This is an offender group. I know some of you have combat stress, too, but the word is still out on how much that contributes to it."

I look out the window and see the guards bringing Miller to the office. "We're going to end early today," I tell them. I assign the homework for next class, "I want you to think about what you contribute to your relationship.

Just focus on you, not what your partner does wrong. Remember, all you have control over is you. And while you're thinking about what you contribute, most all of you here have gone through at least one deployment. I want you to reflect on that."

Everyone groans at the word *reflect*.

I continue, "Yes the *r word*. Reflect and just notice what you feel: hyperaware, jumpy, nightmares, sleep disturbance ... Maybe there are a few things that interfere with intimacy that you brought back with you. Think about it, and I'll see you next group."

Chapter Seven

———◆———

Miller's Voice

I escort the men to the lobby and meet Sergeant Miller with his guards. I greet the men warmly. "Good morning, gentlemen. Why are you here so early? Our appointment isn't until after group. I saw you walk in and ended the group early; I can't do that again. What's up?"

The guard announces, "Colonel Hall ordered us personally to bring him back."

He leans over and whispers in my ear, "He says this guy might be suicidal, and he wants him seen ASAP, ma'am."

Sergeant Miller hears them and responds with irritation, "I am *not* suicidal!" His voice is loud and abrasive.

"You guards can stay here," I tell them. "Miller, come with me."

The guard replies, as if on remote control, "Begging your pardon, ma'am; the colonel said specifically to stay close and to not let this guy out of our sight except behind your office door."

I shrug and head toward my office. "All right then, come with me." They all walk down the corridor to my office, and once again the guards lean their chairs against the door as it closes. I turn to Miller. "Did you use the relaxation and bilateral brain-soothing CDs I gave you?"

He was still standing at attention. "Yes, ma'am."

I notice something different. "What's up? You do seem down today, Miller."

The sergeant sits down and puts his head in his hands.

Still staring down at the floor, he says, "It's my wife. She's going to leave with the kids, and I just can't take it; everyone at work is after me, talking shit about me, and I don't know what I'll do if she leaves me—I just don't know."

"All right, let's start where you hurt the most—your wife, the issues that have separated you, and the infidelity." We get down to business. I always find it is better to be direct because once you start, it becomes easier to work through the issues at hand.

"You say she cheated on you, and then decided to stay. It was when you were deployed, so how did you work out her desire to stay while you were still away—by e-mail, phone?"

Sergeant Miller ponders this for a couple of minutes before speaking. "She decided to stay because I told her something. I told her I had money she didn't know about, so I could take better care of her and my kid. I told her that if she gave me one more chance, I could be the man she wanted me to be."

I'm gaining a better understanding of his internal process. "So, you feel it's your fault she cheated?"

He answers without equivocation, "It *is* my fault, those deployments, being away, not giving her what she needed. Do you know how many people cheat in the corps? They cheat over there; their wives cheat here; it's almost everybody, Doc. But I would have forgiven her; I would have stayed."

I move on. I notice his closed body posture and his nervous twitching, but I press him, "So what happened when you got back?"

Miller really squirms now in his chair, visibly getting more uncomfortable. "I started hearing those f'ing rumors again. This guy in my shop told me she was still screwing around. I told her I was going to get the money soon, but she just couldn't wait. I knew I didn't have the money, but it was all I could tell her to keep her. I just had to try and keep her."

He breaks down sobbing, a broken man. Suddenly his demeanor changes. He looks angry; his jaw visibly tightens; his fists clench, and his breathing gets more rapid. I want him to get in touch with his feelings. Even vomiting out those feelings is releasing them, not holding them in and building them into some kind of suicidal idea.

I encourage him. "Miller, just go ahead and let it out. I know this might seem silly at first, but I want you to look at that empty chair and imagine your wife is sitting there. I want you to tell her what you are feeling right now and how she has hurt you."

Miller turns to the chair; he is visibly uncomfortable. He looks back at me, "I can't do this. It's stupid!"

"Just try it. Get started and it will be fine. Just begin by telling her what she did really hurt you and go from there." This is a Gestalt therapy technique that can be powerful.

Sergeant Miller stutters as he starts speaking. He can hardly get her name out. "Celia, when I knew you were f'ing around on me," (his voice grows timid) "I couldn't believe it. I love you and ..." He breaks down and starts to cry.

I know this is progress; this is real, not some made-up story in his head that lets him stay in some fantasy of how he would like it to be rather than how it really is. I put my hand on his back. "You're doing fine. Let it out."

He talks on through his tears, wiping them off his face as he forces himself on. "I trusted you; I gave you everything, and even after you did what you did I still wanted to forgive you. I really wanted to forgive you."

His cries are loud moans, and I hear the guards outside move away from the door. They probably can't hear exactly what is being said, but they don't want to hear this crying. They must be uncomfortable.

Miller says, "I had a plan; we had a plan; we could have worked it out."

His demeanor changes: he sits upright; his jaw begins to tighten again, and his face looks mean.

"You bitch, you bitch! Everyone hates me, but you are the one who screwed around, not me. No one will talk to me, and now I have nothing, nothing. I just want to see my kids ..." He is hyperventilating. I put my hand on his back. He has learned how to anchor soothing and positive feelings with the relaxation CD I have given him, and my touch automatically begins the process of slowing his breathing down.

I begin to speak to him in a low, soothing tone. "All right, Miller, imagine you are in the garden like the CD taught you; slow your breathing; you've done great. I want you to notice your breathing. Close your eyes; see yourself in the garden relaxed. You can see the clouds floating overhead; you hear the sound of water running in a slow-moving stream, and you are at peace." I tap his arm several times, and his breathing does begin to slow.

"You can open your eyes now; your breathing is calm and slow, and you are present in the room with me, only the two of us. You are feeling relaxed and have a sense of well-being."

Miller is calm now. He looks relieved, as if he feels a release he hasn't been able to accomplish on his own. His face is visibly less tense, and the color returns to his tear-streaked cheeks.

"Wow, I can't believe I did all of that toward a chair. I mean, I don't even know what I said; I just felt so sad and then so angry. Man, I have never done anything like that before! I kind of feel better. I feel tired, though. Is that normal?"

"Normal? I don't know about that word, but you did great. You really responded to that process. I wouldn't do that by yourself, but it shows how you can hold things in that build up and make you feel bad. In your profession you are taught to compartmentalize to stay alive in theater or any dangerous situation. Your life can depend on not accessing emotion in situations that are life-threatening. But, you see, if you hold it in too long it just festers; it eats away at you. Some of those old expressions about getting things off your chest are true. Okay, that's enough for today. How do you feel?"

"I feel lighter, less burdened, I guess. I do feel a little better. I guess she will do whatever she does. I did talk to legal, and I *will* have rights to see my kid, even have him stay with me. Legal said men have more rights today, like you told me."

I am pleased with the progress of the session. This guy does not appear to have pronounced suicidal ideation.

I feel comfortable with his going back to the barracks and setting another appointment to continue the psychotherapy.

I put my hand on his arm again, another anchor of both reassurance and positive regard. "Continue to do the relaxation work, and we will talk in one week unless it is an emergency. But call first, okay?"

Sergeant Miller says, "It was the colonel, not me, who made me come here, but I'm actually glad he did. I have never done anything like this before, Doc. I got to tell you, everybody always wonders what you people do. If you were just going to judge me or automatically know what I am thinking, it would be creepy, but it's not like that at all. I really feel better. Thanks, I'll let Command know, too. Thanks, Doc, I have some hope now."

We get up; I open the door, and he leaves with the guards. I sit down and write my clinical notes, first outlining the anxiety the client felt while promising his spouse money—blood money. Then I tear it up and do another note simply stating the situation, intervention (Gestalt technique), his positive response, and the plan for next week. I write a classic SIRP—Situation, Intervention, Response, and Plan. I don't record any of the other stories he shared with me. I think of what Sam has told me, and I do what I think is clinically appropriate without expanding the words to a point where it might harm the client or involve me in something I want no part of, something completely outside the scope of my work.

Chapter Eight

———◆———

Dinner Talk

The rest of the day is like a movie montage: various people coming and going from my office, clients of different ranks and gender crying or acting stone-faced and rigid, an endless succession of people in pain. I am sitting at my desk writing my last note when the phone rings, and I hear Sam Waters's voice.

"Hello, beautiful, are we on for tonight—Blake, barbecue, picking avocados?"

"Yeah, sure. I don't know about the barbecue, but come for dinner, and we can pick avocados if it isn't too dark."

Sam responds warmly, "Why don't I bring dinner, then we can just hang out, maybe clear off the table and put up the ping-pong net. Didn't you say you have that huge teak table you use for ping-pong?"

I pause for a moment, thinking about it. "That would be great, Sam. Why don't you bring Chinese food? Blake likes Mongolian beef and I like lemon chicken; there's a place right near our house. It's on the corner of Mission and Highway 76. What about seven o'clock?"

Sam replies, "Can we make it six? I have an early brief, and if we start earlier we have more time."

"I'll see you at six then, and I'll shoot you an e-mail with directions," I respond and hang up the phone.

It is late afternoon. The road leading to my Fallbrook avocado ranch is long and winding. My home sits atop a ridge roamed by coyotes, roadrunners, and various other creatures who come out at night. It is surrounded by tall pines where the owls nest, eucalyptus, avocado trees, and fragrant guava trees that surround a labyrinth I use in meditation walking and relaxation. The house is old but exudes a warmth and a feeling of welcome.

The dog barks when he hears Sam punching in the key code at the gate entrance, and I see his NCIS vehicle heading up the driveway. He parks beside the house. I walk out the side door and hug him. Blake is at my side; at seventeen he is poised and protective of his mom. Blake puts his hand out to shake.

"Glad you're here. We hardly ever have anyone visit from the base."

Sam looks past him to the view. "This is amazing! I love it."

He looks up at the towering pine and eucalyptus trees. One eucalyptus tree is so big it looks like the Swiss family Robinson tree house. "Do you have horses too?" he asks us both.

I shake my head. "No, no horses. They have those really cute miniature horses down the street, but I plan on doing a bit of traveling when Blake goes to college next year."

Blake opens the door for us, and we walk into the ranch-style home filled with teak and mango wood furniture. The living room is warm and inviting with flowers and photos: smiling children with Sarah at graduations, ski trips, boating outings, and Hawaiian excursions. I open a bottle of cabernet and hand Sam a goblet. We sit down at the table and look out over the Gird Valley. The view is panoramic.

Blake awkwardly engages Sam. "Hey, Sam—is it okay if I call you Sam, Major Waters?"

"Yes, absolutely," he responds lightheartedly.

"Is it really true that my mom could go to Afghanistan to do counseling if she wanted? I mean, 'cause—no offense, Mom—she's older and she's a civilian?"

"It sounds like you're worried about that, Blake?"

"Hell, yeah! I mean, yeah, I *am* worried about her. When I go away to college I want her to stay safe while I'm gone. I don't think she should go to a war zone. What if I need her? Or she gets hurt or something? She's talked about it 'cause it's so much money and she thinks she could do some good but ... We've never had anyone over from the base that I could ask, so I'm sorry if I'm dumping this on you but I just thought maybe you would know ..."

I interrupt, "Oh, Blake, if you really have a hard time with my going, if you need me around for your first year, we'll talk about it, and I won't go anywhere. I'll be here for you." I take his hand. "Honey, I didn't know it was so much on your mind." I turn to our guest. "Oh, Sam, I'm sorry."

"That's okay. I don't have any kids of my own, so it feels good to be included." We sit at the table and he opens one of the little packages from the restaurant. "Blake, you wanted the Mongolian beef, right?"

Sam hands out the food, and we sit down around the big teak table, talking and eating. After dinner we clear the dishes and set up for ping-pong. We play a few games, and Blake beats everyone every time. He pulls me aside and whispers, "I really like Sam, Mom. I guess I'll let you go on seeing him."

I squeeze his arm and smile. "Thanks, honey," I whisper back in gratitude.

I put on the lights illuminating the property, and Sam and I go outside with a large bag to pick avocados. It is very dark now and moving between the trees, even seeing the fruit, is difficult. The incline of the grove is challenging to navigate, and the potential for falling all the way down to the bottom of the property is high after dark. Sam and I walk along the string of lights running by the road. We clamber down the hill among a clump of avocado trees. I go first, and as I climb down the slope, I step on a rotten avocado, making me lose my balance. I lurch forward, tumbling halfway down the hill, until a tree trunk stops my fall with a thud.

Sam watches this almost in slow motion. He grabs at me, but I am already gone, rolling down the hill in the darkness. He jumps down the hill two steps at a time, a shadowy figure, the light trailing after him. He bounds forward and steps sideways, trying to brace himself. I hear his hard breathing. He strains for a glimpse of where exactly I am, but he can probably barely see the outline of my body on the ground. I am lying quite still against the base of a large fruit-laden tree. I don't make a sound.

Sam finds his words. "Oh, my God, are you all right?" Still no sound, no movement. He kneels beside me, propping himself against the tree, carefully trying to turn me over.

I open my eyes and smile.

Sam doesn't smile back. He pants, "That wasn't

funny! That wasn't funny at all! Are you hurt? Were you pretending? You took a nasty fall!"

I sit up, laughing. He scoops me into his arms—and hits his head on a branch. An avocado falls on me, and I catch it. We both laugh harder. He bends down and kisses me, bringing me back down to the ground, until another avocado falls on our heads, and we hear Blake calling in the distance.

"Mom, Mom, are you down there? Your emergency pager is going off up here. You wanted me to let you know, didn't you? It's really sounding off, over and over ..."

At that moment Sam's phone is buzzing, too, and he looks down and pushes the button on his Blackberry. He holds out a hand to me. "Come on, no more nighttime frolicking in the avocado groves."

We climb back up to the lights. Sam walks down the driveway to return his call, as I hurry into the house with Blake to check my phone. We both run back to meet at the driveway. I throw his coat to him, grab my keys, wave good-bye to Blake, and we both drive our cars off, through the gate and down the winding street.

Chapter Nine

—◆—

Hope Lost

Sam gets back to the base much faster than I do. We both enter through the Camp Pendleton Marine Installation Vandergrift gate, but Sam is NCIS and moves through much faster. I must wait my turn and show my ID in line with the rest. I proceed through the gate to the barracks in area 33; everything has its number on base.

I park alongside Sam's car, and scurry up to the area, which is swarming with NCIS agents, MPs, and people standing about who have been evacuated from the building.

Sam looks up and motions to me.

"Where is he?" I ask him. "Where are his roommates that I'm supposed to talk to? Have they taken Miller away yet?"

He shakes his head. "No, he's still in there. You don't want to see him. Just go back to the rear of the barracks; his roommates are there; the guy's Command wants you to offer them trauma support. I'll catch up to you later."

I walk around the side of the building and see a place

in the bushes where someone has thrown up. Cigarette smoke, men's voices as I round the corner.

I approach them. "Are you gentlemen Sergeant Miller's roommates? Who found him?"

One of the men steps forward. "Sergeant Greco, ma'am. I found him. I walked in and he was just hanging there."

"Then what happened?" I can feel the emotion in my throat, I only saw Miller briefly, but he cared about his family, his wife, his career. Miller was one of the decent guys among so many indecent characters who just wanted to bleed him dry and discard him like he didn't matter, like his life was worth nothing.

Sergeant Greco speaks nonchalantly, with little or no emotion appropriate to the terrible event that has just happened, the death of a marine—and the death of a roommate. "Well, I saw him there, and I guess I went and told someone."

I think that sounds odd. Not odd that he would try to find help, but combined with his lack of emotion, I feel it is odd that he didn't try to cut him down and revive him if possible. "Did you try to help Miller?" I ask. "You didn't mention checking to see if he was alive or doing CPR until help arrived. You didn't shout out and try to help—or did you?"

The marine just stands there with a look on his face that says, "Why the hell was a shrink asking him that?"

"I don't know, ma'am; I just knew he was dead, that's all."

I persist. It is not in my purview to do that, in fact NCIS would be furious about my asking that type of question, but it just blurts out like something important I must ask. I am supposed to be doing a standard critical incident debrief, provide normalization for those affected, offer counseling later, and just check in to determine the degree of trauma to witnesses. But these guys don't seem traumatized. Sometimes the reaction comes later, and marines are taught to compartmentalize their feelings under the extreme stress such a traumatic event brings, but there is a difference here. I can't know for sure what it is, but something just doesn't feel right about this group. The three other marines are standing there looking casually around. They show no emotion.

I speak to the group: "I was asked to come over here to do some crisis counseling for those of you who were affected either by finding Sergeant Miller, knowing him, or being affected by his death."

Sergeant Greco says, "I don't know what you mean, ma'am. It's nice enough for you to come all the way over here, but we don't need you, do we? Do any of you need to talk to this 'counselor?'" His tone is sarcastic and has a note of disrespect. The others shake their heads, and there is a long moment of uncomfortable silence.

I have never heard this before either. Even if people don't want to talk, they generally like having a counselor stick around for a while or talk about the weather or something that has nothing to do with the event that brought them together.

I speak cautiously, "Okay, then, usually in this kind of situation someone benefits from at least talking about what happened, how he was found, concerns, maybe even 'feelings,' but clearly that isn't the case here. Oh, did one of you get sick to your stomach? I almost stepped in some vomit outside over there."

Sergeant Greco is borderline insolent. "I think I can speak for everyone here, ma'am. Ain't nobody got sick over anything that happened here."

I nod and turn to leave; I can hear their muffled voices as I round the corner and run into Sam. I am grateful for the presence of a friend.

"That was weird. I mean, what wouldn't be weird in a situation like this, but I go out on a lot of these types of calls lately, and here no one was saying they were upset or needed to talk, or even said they knew him but he was a jerk, and they feel bad about the last thing they said to the guy ... just nothing, and no one mentioned that they tried to check to see if they could help the guy. I mean, your brother is hanging there and the first reaction is not to check if he is still alive or cut him down. That's weird. No critical incident debriefing needed at all or wanted; that is odd for a situation where someone took his own life. And *that* is weird, because there was no hint of suicidal ideation. I just saw the guy."

Sam interrupts me, "I thought you couldn't tell me if you were seeing him ..."

I am not amused by his remark. "Well, I can sure as hell tell you now, because he's dead and NCIS is assuming this case, aren't they?"

Sam replies, a bit put off by my abruptness, "Yeah, actually we are, because it doesn't look like he had any way to actually hang himself. He was hoisted up there all right, but look, there is nothing to get him up there, nothing close enough to stand on nearby, nothing other than that rope, and look at the length. He also has a needle puncture bruise on his right arm; we need to find out if he had any medical treatment, if he went to medical today. We aren't gonna know until the medical examiner tells us, but I bet he wasn't even killed here. I think he was put up there; maybe to send a message, and if your impression of that group back there is any indicator, we have a bit of a mess on our hands and a lot of unanswered questions.

We couldn't find that dirty little bag he said he always had with him—you know, the one he used to carry his money everywhere in Iraq."

"Why are you telling me all this? I don't need to know this; my job is done now. If those guys need additional counseling—like they can't sleep, notice their appetite has changed, feel worse—but otherwise I go back to my little world."

Sam doesn't stop. "I don't think this is over for you, Fox." (He always calls me by my last name when it's something serious at work.) "Do you think he took the money or not? There are going to be people asking you that very question. There's a lot of money at stake here. It's not going to go away; in fact, it just got a whole lot more interesting, and you are definitely a part of this."

Sam has never talked to me like this. He is straining to make me understand. He cares about me.

"Everyone knows you saw him; he walked around talking about how great you were. That may sound good, but if anyone thinks he told you about the money or, God forbid, where the money is, you are in trouble. I know the CO is going to want to talk to you; Christ, maybe even the general, even if you only saw him a few times."

Twice? I suddenly became aware of how much I have been monitored. "How do you know how many times I've seen him?"

"That's just a figure of speech. Just be prepared; first thing tomorrow have it in shape. The NCIS investigative team will be there with their own copy machine."

I walk away, waving my hand over my head. "See you later. Thanks for tonight; the Chinese food was great. Blake told me on the down low that he really liked you." I really like you, too, I think.

I get in my car and drive back home. I am tired. I pull up to my property gate, push the remote button in my car, and disappear into the darkness. I feel safe at home.

Chapter Ten

---◆---

Growing Voice

Like every business morning, the clock hits 5:30 and I'm up, making the lunches; the row of orange lights embedded in the ceiling shine down on the counter. I lean over and give the old dog a piece of turkey; he bites my finger by accident as he snatches it.

Blake comes in, grabs his lunch, kisses me on the cheek. "Hey, Mom, I'm making tacos for dinner, and if you want, Sam can come back over."

"Naw, I want to just hang with you tonight. Sam is nice, but getting those college applications done is important, and we need to get on that, right?" He smiles and agrees, glad I remembered his priority.

I grab my work briefcase and my coffee and head out, calling back to Blake, "Have a good day! Love you!" as I open the door and throw in my bag. I try never to start a day without telling him that. Each day I see the worst of relationships—the beatings and abuse, the backhands and the head butts.

Today will not be The Day; the job will not get me

to the point of quitting, of walking out. It's the mantra—
every morning, every night. Not today. Not me. Not this
way. I am stronger than this. I wish I didn't have to be.
I stop myself for a moment and recall the 91st Psalm—
"under His wings you will find refuge," I am beginning to
realize that perhaps I need to look for strength within the
light of my faith and not the rejection of the darkness of
the depravity that surrounds me. I have learned that you
can't solve the problem at the level of the problem. One
must rise above. Stay grounded by rising above.

Arriving at the counseling clinic, I begin to prepare
for the group. I'm excited, to be honest. I want to see
the change, the development. They are coming along,
and some might even get out of here a little bit better.
When I'm ready, I go down the hall toward the group
counseling room. I hear running steps behind me, quick
trotting with a slight gimp, and know immediately to turn
around and greet the dour face of our secretary. Her gait
is unmistakable; much like the ever-present indifference
on her face.

"Doc Fox," she begins, "the investigative team is
here with their copier; there was a death on base last night
of a client you saw, and they need ..."

I am way ahead of her. I interrupt her with a wave
toward my office. "The file is on my desk, locked in my
office, please give it to them. They're welcome to copy
what they need. All the files should be there, but I really
must be getting back to work." Someone had died last
night, but it was business as usual here.

The administrative secretary is surprised. "Great,
thank you. How did you have that file out already?" Her
indifference gives way to what seems like concern. The
job has beaten her down, too, I know, but I haven't thought
about what did it to her. I guess it was greeting hostile

clients daily that didn't want to be there, bureaucratic wrangling of clinicians, Commands, and structure. It must be hard for her to get anything done. I reply as warmly as I can muster: "I was there last night. I was called out by Command to do a critical incident debrief with his roommates at the barracks, and I anticipated Command needing to know what I was doing with him in therapy. He had no suicidal ideation that last time I saw him; he was just a poor chap whose wife cheated on him when he was deployed, and he really wanted to work it out. Pretty straightforward really, but he gave me no indication that he would harm himself."

The secretary was obviously interested in the case, but I couldn't say any more, and her interest trailed off. "Thanks, Doc Fox. I really appreciate working with you; you are so respectful of me, of the clients. Some of the therapists here just aren't." She begins to waver, but I cut her off before she starts crying. Everyone seems on the verge of tears around here.

"You work hard, and if we work as a team it serves the patients much better. I'll be in group if you need me." We walk by reception on the way to the group room. The NCIS team is gathered not far from the door and appears to be loitering, as if it were an element of training, and the core aspect of one of the lengthier classes at Naval Criminal Investigation Service Academy. I notice as I walk up to greet them that Sam is not among them. He would have been with the officers and not gathering the files.

Without small talk, and with no interest in discussing any matters beyond their cases, I walk into the group room at counseling services. Setting the files down on the table, I look up after a pause. "Last time we talked briefly about how combat stress can play a role in screwing up your relationships. (That's a clinical term.)"

I don't smile with that last comment. As a clinician here, I know that even a smile can give away the power over a group, that even the slightest appearance of weakness among warriors may lead to a power struggle. With new additions every week, and new cases every day, I must maintain control, which is ironic considering that this group got here via incidents related to the abuse of power and control. Often, it's up to the men to keep each other in line.

Everyone laughs, and I continue, "Tatum, I think you were having a reaction to what we were saying. Haven't you said you experience some of the combat stress-related symptoms we have described?" Tatum looks surprised to be called out right from the start, but it's good to keep them on their toes.

"Yes, ma'am, I do all of it. But what you said before about being here voluntarily, that ain't true for us. We got here because our Commands sent us; they say it's 'cause we took an 'aggressive part in an incident which resulted in an arrest,' but that isn't true for some of us, especially me. I came in on my own and reported what happened. Some people just want to get help, but instead they get all messed up, have to go before a board and tell our business and wind up in group. You say it's not a punishment, but it feels like a punishment."

He was right. Of course, it would feel like a punishment. It felt like going to court, being found guilty of a crime, and being sentenced to rehabilitation. At some level this was true. Except in the civilian world the judge would have sentenced him to a much worse fate—a fifty-two-week program that is fraught with shame and blame.

The corpsman sits up straight and cuts in. "I did that, too; you're talking about me exactly! I came in for anger management and wound up here because I told them about the fight over the remote, and BAM, here I am. It's bullshit; it's dangerous coming here! I should never have said what happened at all." He finishes with almost a whine, which can spread like wildfire in a group like this.

Of course, the next would be Booth; with perfect timing he rushes the group with, "Bam! That's like that Emeril guy. I like that guy." He smiles to himself, and the rest around the table laugh. Some jeer, but most agree with him. It's a break in the discussion, but every dark moment needs a little comic relief.

I smile for a second, and the group relaxes. "Oh God, Booth." As I begin to move the conversation along, General Markham opens the door and pokes his head in. Immediately all the service members leap to their feet, salute, and keep their bodies at rigid attention. When a general enters a room, it becomes his, immediately.

With the clear authority of a man used to giving commands and having those commands followed instantly, General Markham looks directly at me and says, "Doc Fox, I am terribly sorry to intrude upon your group." He glances around, "At ease, gentlemen." No one moves. They stay at rigid attention. General Markham simply disbands the group with a few words. "Your group has ended for today, gentlemen. I am sure the doctor will see to it that everything is in order and you receive full credit for the day. Doc Fox, I will give you a few minutes to end the group, give assignments if needed. Meet me in your office ASAP; I will be there waiting."

I think about that for a second. Something is up, but I don't have time to mull it over. I look past him and see Smith right behind him. He is waving at me, while the other men in the group roll their eyes and try to ignore him. I work within the military structure, I know whom

I serve, and whom I cannot ignore, at least for now. In a civilian world this would not have happened; I would be the authority setting the boundaries, but not here. This is not MY world, this is theirs, and even though I don't have a rank on my shoulders or a cubbyhole in the command structure, the authority still demands I step in line.

"General, I will dismiss the group immediately and meet you in my office."

"Thank you. I trust it won't take too long." He turns to leave without another word or recognition to the group. This never happens; a general never pops into a domestic violence offender group.

I turn to the group and speak to Smith. "Go back to the secretary and reschedule your appointment. I'll need to meet with you another time." He looks distraught, and a sigh leaves his lips, but he leaves. I turn to the group as the door closes. "All right," I begin, but I am suddenly interrupted.

"Dr. Fox, I swear I know that guy ..." The corpsman trails off, but clearly, he is thinking about the young man who has just left. The expression on his face is a grimace; whoever he thinks Smith is, it's not a good person.

I should have listened—I know that now, but I didn't know then, and a general was calling me to talk. I didn't have time for my misgivings, and I had to press forward. Rebuffing the corpsman, I said in passing, "You mean the general? I bet you do." My mind was already racing ahead to my meeting with him.

"No, I mean that guy who was behind him waving at you, the guy you told to reschedule."

I feel pressured. I'm not paying attention to him. The general must come first.

"You heard the general; we're stopping here. We

aren't going to have time to do check-in today. Gather everything together; you're dismissed."

"OO-rah! OO-rah!" the group is muttering together as they start to leave. Some are eager to go. Leaving early is the one treat these guys have. But others, the ones who want to get better, who have been in the group the longest, aren't quite as enthusiastic. As they begin to file out, I have a thought. It's going to help bring the group back next time, and hopefully give the newbies something to think about.

I turn and hold up a hand. "You're going to have an extra homework assignment."

The group groans, rolls their eyes, but listens.

"You guys and gal have put so much focus on what you don't want, what is wrong, and how terrible it is and was …"

"It does suck," Carson chimes in, diffident, without malicious intent.

"I hear you"—and I did hear him—"so I am giving you an opportunity to declare what you want. You know, with all of your experiences, if you see it, you can have it; if you believe you can, you can. In your work, if you see the mission accomplished it will be. So, I ask you, what do you want? What would a loving relationship look like?"

They call this type of assignment "solution focused." What would it look like? But remember the infamous statement from AA that applies to all twelve-step programs: insanity is doing the same thing over and over, having the same relationship behaviors, and expecting a different outcome. So why does it always need to be said, and why do the behaviors keep being repeated?

Martinez responds to this assignment enthusiastically,

"So you want us to dream, to imagine what we really want?"

I nod my head. "Yes, but the work is to imagine what beliefs you need to change to get it. Just like we tell you the focus of the group is on you; the changes must come from within you. Not just dumping the old relationship and moving on to the next relationship, because your demons will follow you. They live in your head and come roaring out from your heart." I see just how true that is now. "Oh, and over the next few groups I want you to bring something in that represents what you want, something real that can help you focus and keep going to get it. Like a picture, music, or an object, something real. As we have time, we will reflect on these items and get a better understanding of how you can create the future, the relationships you want. You must see it, visualize it before you can make it real in your life. See you next time! Oh, and, Goodman, if you sit here looking depressed but not talking, looking at people with that piercing stare but not contributing to the group, well, let me put it to you this way—you must talk next time, or you get kicked out, and you don't want to deal with the ramifications of that. Do you?"

Goodman has been sitting in the corner just staring down the entire group. He nods his skinned head in response.

Carson turns to Martinez and speaks softly, "What's your Command and your MOS?"

Martinez whispers back, "That's like asking your sign." They laugh. Everyone begins exiting the room. Carson and Martinez are talking and walking out side by side. They leave the building together, and for an instant I can see them through the window as they stop at the edge of the park near the building. I wish I were close enough to overhear them.

Carson says, "We got dismissed early, so do you have time to just sit and talk?"

Martinez agrees, "Yes, how about that bench over there. I got a little time to kill." They walk closely together, a clear sweet chemistry between them, and they sit down on a bench underneath a pepper tree near a pond. There are ducks and herons standing nearby; it is quiet and serene. That such a place exists here is testimony to the will of the human spirit to create nature and beauty even in the presence of war.

"So why did you become a marine?"

She takes a deep breath. "My great-grandfather, he fought in World War Two. He used to tell me stories about the world, about getting out there. My mom didn't; she just stayed in East LA, knowing my dad was going out on her, but saying she just couldn't leave. She still just takes it. He never hits her like I got with my husband, but she just takes it, and I see her fading away. I couldn't do it. You know, I want more, so I joined, and I like it. I feel good about myself, about making corporal."

Martinez looks down at her watch and says to Carson, "Do you mind if we start walking? I don't live far from here. We can just walk that way if it's okay with you. If I get back earlier, I can get my daughter out of day care and spend more play time with her. My schedule has been so crazy right now, and my first sergeant doesn't care if *you have children. He says if you are a marine that comes first, no matter what your babysitter schedule is. Is it okay if we walk and talk?"*

Carson responds, "Sure." He is happy to walk with her; he feels a kinship between them. Searching for something to talk about, he asks, "What do you think you'll bring in next week to group?"

Martinez already knows what she is going to do. "I have this cassette tape that my mom gave me of a song my great-grandmother listened to while her husband was away at war. It was Christmastime, and, like, they didn't even know if he would make it back. He sent her the vinyl of that song, and she played it over and over. Later my mom found it on cassette and gave it to me. Angel and me listen to it a lot 'cause that's the kind of relationship I want. You just long for that person and dream about them returning to you. There's no cheating, no jealousy, no hurting each other, 'cause I think that's what love is, just believing that you will stay connected, be able to get back to each other no matter what you know, you believe. I guess it's faith."

They arrive at her small base housing unit. Martinez continues, "This is my house, you want to come in and hear it? I want to play it for you if you want to hear it."

Carson looks around, thinking of some of the things he has heard about her estranged husband. He is worried.

"Yeah, but I don't know if I should come in your house. Where is your crazy ass husband?

"There's a Military Protective Order; he has to stay in the barracks. I stay here because of the baby, and because he was in the brig before, they let me. It's okay. I want you to hear the song."

They walk in. It's a small base housing apartment:

drab, a sagging futon couch, a broken coffee table, a smashed stereo. Carson notices the broken stereo and asks, "What are you going to play it on? Your stereo looks trashed; is that from you and ... "

Martinez ignores his question at first; she is still immersed in her vision of what she would really like to see in her life. "You just long for that person who will love you and not hurt you. It's so simple, but I just can't seem to get there yet."

She walks past the living room filled with the broken evidences of domestic violence. "Don't look at that; come in here," she says, as they walk through the old war zone. She leads him to the back of the house, to the nursery, and pushes open the door that is hanging by its hinges. The room is pink and lovely, with comforters, a little chair with a princess table, and a rocking horse. A Little Tykes tape recorder and player sits on the table.

Martinez points to it. "This looks like a toy, but it really works; it records and plays back cassettes. Let me show you." She puts the old cassette in the little recorder and pushes the big red button. The John Pizzeria version of "I'll Be Home for Christmas" begins to play, and a smile slowly grows on Martinez's face. She begins to dance with her hands held up in waltz position. She floats around the small pink room. "This is just like how Dancing with the Stars *would do it. We like to pretend when we see that show."*

Carson laughs and makes a slight bow. Martinez curtseys in reply; both in cammies and boots, they stand smiling at each other—clumsy yet delicate, respectful and sweet. He takes her arm elegantly and leads her in a waltz around the nursery. Midway through, the song is interrupted by the voice of a three-year-old singing to her doll.

Instantly, Martinez breaks away, very upset. She cries out, "Oh, my God! She didn't! I can't believe this! She recorded over my song! I just wanted this one thing for myself! It's my hope; it's my someday." She kneels and takes out the tape. Tears swell in her eyes, but she doesn't give way to them. Carson tries to comfort her, but she pulls away and sets the recorder down on the princess table.

Martinez gets very stiff; her manner changes abruptly. "You better go. I'm sorry you saw me like this. I'll suck it up." She wipes the tears away. "I can't bring this to class next week. That figures. I had the perfect thing; this really is what I wanted to bring; I knew it right away, but nothing ever goes right for me. I thought this one time, but, no, even that's screwed up."

Carson is at a loss to know what to do. "Maybe you can find another tape ..."

She turns on him. "Are you kidding? You can't even buy cassette tapes any more. Just go, okay?"

Carson, still trying to help, says, "Well, maybe it's on a CD. Songs like that have been recorded by lots of people. Maybe you ... maybe we can find it."

Chapter Eleven

———◆———

Money Talks, Bullshit Walks

General Markham interrupting my group is extraordinary. A general visiting counseling services never happens. The senior leadership avoids the counseling office. With the events of the previous night, the general's presence indicated something was up. As I enter my office, General Markham, Sam, Colonel Hall, and Staff Sergeant Gilmore all are sitting around my desk. I move through the doorway, turn my back to them, and sigh to myself to keep my composure. I know I will need to control any emotion. I close the door, and as I move toward the desk, they mute their conversation and stand.

"All right, gentlemen, how may I help you?"

General Markham speaks first. "We have a dead marine, Doc, and we have a lot of questions that need to be answered—now. You were one of the last people to see him alive, and I need to know what your assessment of this marine was. Do you think he was capable of harming himself?"

He wants a reply. I haven't had have time to check

my files, but I respond instantly in my deepest monotone voice. I always use this tone with the military. If I showed signs of softness on base, I'd be eaten alive. "Sir, I understand the gravity of the situation. As you can see by my notes—" I begin to explain but am quickly interrupted by Markham.

He grimaces and tightens his fist. Clearly, he is under stress, but to his credit, he controls his anger. He is doing his best not to take it out on me. If I ever speak with him after this case, I will be sure to acknowledge it. "Hell, I can't see a damn thing by your notes. That's the problem; you just focus in those notes on his situation, intervention, response, and plan. The damn SIRP! I hate that format." He begins to get off track a bit, but quickly regains his original thought, this time with a bit less harshness in his tone. He sounds tired, almost sad, but still very, very serious.

"I just got the feeling that this guy was cheated on, was alienated, but not suicidal, and is trying to go on with his life with these relaxation things you gave him—deep breathing and all that crap, pardon the expression. Is that really all?"

"Yes, sir," I reply. "Those were the issues involved. I understand that the SIRP format is brief, but that is protocol, and he was cooperative, mildly depressed, but appeared to have a rapport with me, building trust, utilizing the relaxation techniques. I only saw him twice. He had no SI, suicidal ideation, indicated. I really would not have thought he would harm himself and certainly not by hanging, sir. But we are surprised daily. He did have some combat stress, but seemed to benefit from the stress reduction techniques. I am sorry it ended this way. I really am sorry. I think he really could have gotten better. And I was surprised by his roommates, too. There was no outward sign of reaction by his roommates to finding him or to him apparently taking his own life. I do a lot of critical incident debriefing and that was unusual. Is that all, sir?"

While it is always important to be brief and to the point with COs, you never want to say too much, and you need to get out after you state your peace. I feel that there is something more here. The gnawing feeling from the previous night returns.

General Markham looks at the group of officers. "Do you have any more questions, Hall? Waters? Gilmore? Fox, do you mind if we commandeer your office for a bit?"

Commandeer my office? My work? "No problem. I must see a patient, but I can use another therapy room. If I can be of any further assistance in this matter ... Have you notified the family? I know his wife and ..." But I am interrupted again before I can finish.

Colonel Hall cuts me off with a wave of the hand—a dismissive gesture taken right out of the 1950s. "Yes, ma'am, that's taken care of."

"If you will excuse me then, I have a patient waiting. Please contact me if you have any questions." As I close the door, I can hear Colonel Hall say, "Thank you for your cooperation, Doctor F ..."

Chapter Twelve

Command Demands

I walk out of the room to the reception, meet Smith, and lead him to another therapy room, but my mind is on the general commandeering my office for his meeting.

General Markham begins the discussion. "So, what do we have here? A dead marine who may have stolen a hell of a lot of money; what looks like a suicide but isn't, and a group of marines who look guilty as hell. Sam, what does NCIS think?"

The phone rings and Sam answers it. He turns to General Markham and Staff Sergeant Gilmore, nods his head, and hangs up. He addresses the group, "Miller was probably injected with a stimulant like epinephrine. The

ME just confirmed it. His cause of death was not hanging; he died before being hung up there. His heart stopped prior to the hanging. Any medical officer could have gotten their hands on that information. Hell, any corpsman ... Was there a corpsman in that group we interviewed at the barracks after his death?"

"No, he had no corpsmen as roommates. Who would he have seen at BAS? Has he had any contact with anyone from medical? Does he have any friends who are corpsmen?"

Staff Sergeant Gilmore responds, "He did go to see the medical officer pretty often, headaches, but nothing recently, and he had no friends at all. Even his wife hasn't been around the last few days. She went back with their child to visit her family somewhere in the South, Georgia, I think."

Waters takes charge, "Well, at least we have our first real understanding. Doc Fox was right; he wasn't suicidal. Now we just need to take it inside. Nobody signed on the base last night to go to that area, no civilians; this has to be one of us."

Sam continues, "The medical examiner established the probable time of death as early in the afternoon. He confirmed it as a homicide, not a suicide. The doc was right about that; he didn't do himself in, and his roommates either know more or did it themselves. We have them over in the interrogation room now. At the very least it could be a code red; someone taking this guy out. Ever since that Jack Nicholson movie—what was it? We found vomit outside the barracks; maybe that's nothing or maybe it was the killer. We need to move on this fast."

General Markham smiles for a second. "It was A Few Good Men. *I love that movie."*

All at once they all say at the same time, "You can't handle the truth!"

General Markham brings them all back. "You really think it could be that? Well, there was all that talk about him; a lot of people hated him, thought he had all that cash. All those people around him died on those convoys trying to get that blood money to those freaking hadjies ... . You did not hear me say that."

They all nod their heads.

"You take care of this, all of you; this is priority, and I want zero press on this, understand?"

They all stand as he leaves the room. As they file out and exit the building, Sam stops at the desk and leaves a note.

Smith and I finish and walk together to the exit. I tell him, "That was a great session; I think you're really making progress. Keep on doing the guided imagery to relax yourself, and the combat flashbacks should continue to fade, and you should start feeling more like your old self was before theater."

Smith speaks patronizingly, "Thanks, Doctor Fox. I don't know how to thank you, but could you just call over to the BAS and let them know I still need my meds?"

I turn to him, thinking something about what he just said was not right. "I thought you were being seen at deployment health?"

He reacts with anger. "No, they didn't get it. They

were assholes over there. Last time I went there they had these goons take me to the hospital; they wanted me to go into rehab."

I stare at him, puzzled, "What? Nobody told me. How many places have you been seen? How many people?"

Corpsman comes up behind me and peers at Smith, who abruptly turns to leave. "Gotta go, I'll see you next week."

After he is gone, the corpsman says, "Here's my homework from last week. I *do* know that guy. That's the guy, Smith. Our medical officer flagged his chart as drug-seeking. He comes in the BAS every week to try to get more drugs—painkillers for his back, Clonipin for his anxiety—he's a mess. You know he is totally f'ing with you, Doc. You know what his MOS is?"

"I told you I can't talk about him to you. I told you I didn't know his MOS or his Command when you asked me before. I could look it up, I guess."

The corpsman speaks with disdain, "Don't bother checking him out; I'll tell you. He's not a grunt or a gunner, or a f'ing artillery man, not even motor T. He's a f'ing POG—an admin f'ing POG. I'm just saying what goes around comes around. People like that deserve what they get for betraying Marine Corps values."

"I do think what goes around comes around, but maybe you're wrong about that guy. His MOS, his job was admin—or a POG, person other than grunt, as you call it—but he volunteered for deployment and was put in an MOS as a lead gunner. You know that happens a lot. People get pulled and wind up in something they never thought they would do, because of the need."

Corpsman won't give it up. "That might be true, but it's not true for him; he's an addict. He wasn't no front gunner, or back gunner, or any gunner, and if he is f'ing with people—lying and crap—he is going to get it. He isn't the only one; anyone who cheats, steals, is going to get found out. That guy hurt his back in a power-lifting competition in Allasad, not from an IED. Not from anything related to combat. People hate that guy. Rumors are that he sells H and meth, too."

"So, what would you have me do, corpsman? That's what they call you, corpsman, isn't it? You are the real doc here. People trust you. I hear the grunts won't see an MD before you say it's okay to trust them. Is that true?"

"Yeah, I guess that's true," corpsman replies.

"So, do you judge the people you treat?"

He protests adamantly, "No, but that's different. That's in theater. They depend on me. They're my brothers, and we're fighting together. I trust them, and they trust me. That's real. That POG isn't real. He's a poser and worse— he's a poser wanting drugs for pain related to something he didn't fight for."

"So, let me stop you there. I don't judge him. I look at him and see pain. I see someone who has no idea how really messed up he is. Until he goes to rehab and beyond, he won't have a clue. He'll keep running his game and may even die while doing it, but the pain part is real. The psychic pain is real, and that's what I treat. Some people from this group you're in ask me that, too."

"Ask you what?"

"They ask me how I can stand being with people that hurt other people—people they love, people they declared they would love and cherish forever. So, if I couldn't get beyond the judgment of you guys in a domestic violence offender group, if I didn't think people could change, I couldn't and shouldn't be here. Shaming people has never been therapeutic. Confronting people with questions is different. Provoking empathy, asking someone to put themselves in someone else's shoes, that's important. Do you think someone can change if they don't feel sorry for what they did? If they don't feel empathy for the ones they hurt?"

The corpsman looks strangely at me, then turns and leaves.

I finish for the day and head for home. I'm tired and looking forward to putting this behind me, sitting on my deck and just listening to the birds and watching the sunset. I haven't heard from Sam this evening; he must be completely absorbed in this case. I think about the day, and I just can't figure out what happened to that poor young man who died. It's sad. That's common; there are a lot of sad stories on base these days, far away from combat on the battlefield, yet just as dangerous. The mine fields are mental here and harder to see. Military life is a harsh life for both active-duty service members and civilian workers.

Chapter Thirteen

————◇————

Say What You Mean, Mean What You Say

The next group begins, as they always do, with the check-in. Each member states what got them into an offender group. I look around to make sure everyone is accounted for, and begin, "We didn't do check-in last time, so we are starting with that, then we'll break, and then I'll have you present and turn in your solution-focused homework on the nature of the relationship you want for the future.

"Let's just jump in. Tatum, you're up. Remember not to blame your wife or say what she did. This is about you; she's not here. We can only work on your issues as they relate to domestic violence."

Tatum says, "She is too here. She just sits out there and watches, so she knows where I am. Ain't that controlling?"

Everyone turns to look out the window. They burst out laughing, and Lamar just shakes his head.

"Well, like I said, we know partners do things, but

this is about you. We can't make spouses get treatment; we can only be thankful that the military makes it possible to encourage you—or let's just say it like it is—make you come here and look at your stuff."

People are still laughing and pointing out the window, where we can all see her sitting outside.

Tatum launches into check-in, "Okay, my name is Lamar. My wife's name is Shawna. We have no kids; no alcohol was involved. What got me here was arguing with my wife again about money and bar-bee-kew-in' ..."

Everybody laughs.

Tatum continues, "The money is what started it. She spent a lot while I was deployed, not in a bad way, but a lot. But it was the bar-bee-kew that was really the problem; that's what got me here."

Fewer men laugh this time, but it was still there.

Tatum is undaunted. "It's 'cause she knows I can't take that smell; I told her I can't take that smell." He wrings his hands and shakes his head from left to right.

I come over to Tatum and put my hand on his shoulder. "Tatum!" I wave my hands in front of his face.

He jerks to a stop. Without missing a beat, he continues, "I'm over there, and she's spending my money."

"You don't need to tell us that, just the actions, physical and emotional abuse, that got you here."

Booth won't let it go. He yells out, "Hell, no, I want to know why she can't cook barbeque. Man, I love barbeque. If I had somebody cook it for me, man, I'd love it with greens."

Tatum cuts in, "I can. I'll tell *him*, Doc; he's a grunt; he's gonna understand."

I go along with it just because he is participating.

"All right, but this can't be about blaming Shawna, okay?"

Tatum starts, "Okay. So, you guys know I am motor T. I ain't nobody kicking in doors; we just take care of the seven-tons, you know." Everyone nods in understanding, and Booth nods emphatically.

Tatum goes on, "So why are we motor T guys always there first?"

I want to know what he means. "Where first? What are you talking about?"

"Man, we are there first. We get the call, an IED, a firefight, a seven-ton goes down, and we gotta go and get the vehicle before those hadjies take our stuff, before the looters. But we get there first before them, before they can get the bodies, our guys. Those morgue guys are supposed to be there first, get out the guys, our guys, you know. I care about those guys, but that's not our job. We get there, over and over, and all you know is that burning smell. I got so I could smell that a mile away, no bullshit. I would be driving closer and closer and those hadjies shooting at us, and I don't even care. I just care about that damn smell. You can't get it out of your clothes, your hair, off your fingers. I'd just roll up and hide behind those seven-tons and wait for the morgue guys and backup, listening to AC/DC 'Highway to Hell' through my earbuds. Not caring if I was shot or killed or nothing. I just wanted to stop smelling that smell. I can't tell my wife that. She doesn't want to know that stuff anyway, it scares her. I just can't get near barbeque. It smells like that to me; it brings me back there; it makes my skin crawl; it makes me want to throw up, run away, or do anything just not to smell, hear, and feel those things … So, I try to tell her, and she just doesn't get it. She thinks I'm being picky 'cause our friends all love barbeque and getting together."

Booth pats his shoulder. "Man, that sucks. I know

what you mean, but I never felt it that bad."

I understand; it makes sense. "Tatum, have you been to hospital postdeployment clinic? This is what combat stress looks like. You need to get help for it."

"Yeah, yeah. I'm just gonna do my check-in. I yelled at her, called her an ungrateful bitch, bad wife, stupid, lazy; I grabbed her purse. It didn't come off her wrist, and I yanked it. She's real little, and she flew across the room with it, she landed on the floor, and I held her down with my hand to her chest to calm her down."

They snicker.

Goodman finally speaks up. "You can't calm her down by putting your hands on her, man, and if your child sees it that breaks the law, and it breaks his heart, too, and he will never love you again. Man, it's just over; it's never gonna get better."

The whole group is quiet.

Carson seems shy. He's obviously uncomfortable listening to the story and asks, "Do I really have to listen to this?"

Martinez is sitting next to him and leans over, putting her hand on his arm. "You'll get used to it." She covers his hand with hers. Booth notices. She catches his eye and quickly takes her hand away.

I encourage him, "Go on, and then what happened?"

Tatum is serious, and his jaw noticeably tightens as he talks. "I took her purse and wallet; then I took the debit card and credit card. Her wrist had a friction burn; two of her ribs were broken, and I took her phone, so she couldn't call 911, which I now know is a felony. I don't know who called the police, but I was arrested and spent five days in jail. My Command also made me give her back the debit card with access to my money. They said it was a marine order to safeguard spouses and families. I'm the man; I'm the head of my house, and I should decide when to give her what I think is right. And another thing, I told her never to cook barbeque, and she did that night."

Booth tries to diffuse the emotional tension, "Well, I guess I ain't gonna ask you to eat at the ranch house tonight."

Everyone laughs, and the group says in unison, "OO-rah!"

"So, Tatum, what did you bring in to tell what you want now?"

"I just want to be like I used to be, fun, wanting to be with my brother. I just want to feel like myself, like I'm not in quicksand, drowning, crying, skin crawling. I want Shawna there like when we first got married. I know it's me; it's not her. I brought in this picture of us at our wedding right before I deployed the first time, and I brought this guided imagery CD 'cause I play it over and over. I do see myself in the garden, peaceful like, near a river, calm, relaxed. I see it every day, and that's what I want; I want to find my way back to Shawna, how it used to be, how I used to be."

"Great job, Tatum, thanks," I say. "Okay, Booth, after that ranch house barbeque comment you have our attention." But before Booth can start, the secretary appears at the door and interrupts.

"I'm sorry, Dr. Fox, for interrupting, but there is someone on the phone who says it's an emergency."

I get up and before leaving turn to the group.

"You guys start on your homework. You take the power and control wheel; that's the handout that has you look at behaviors related to domestic abuse like isolation, financial control, physical abuse, intimidation, and make a list of all the things you have contributed to the relationship to get you here today. I will be back as soon as I can."

I walk down the corridor to the secretary's desk and pick up the phone. On the line is Commanding Officer Watkins. "Doc Fox, I understand I have interrupted your group. I apologize for that. I just spoke with several friends of the deceased service member who came to see you, and they told me he disclosed some things to you that could have security relevance, and I think I might need to debrief you."

The presumption was now that I knew something more than I should. "Debrief me, sir? I am not a service member, and I don't need to tell you anything unless he reports domestic violence to me or some criminal activity or substance abuse. I don't need to say that he just focused on his wife, sir. He was really upset about her infidelity; that is what we were working on, and I am sure you also must have found the stress reduction and guided imagery CD I gave him to provide training in self-soothing and bilateral stimulation. Will you be returning that to me?"

As I finish Commanding Officer Watkins chimes in with a stern voice, but with some relief. "If he didn't share anything related to his activities in Iraq, I don't need to speak with you further, Doctor." He hangs up abruptly.

I know I shouldn't take it personally; it is always that way on base. If someone is finished with you, it will always be abrupt. I put down the phone and ask the secretary, "Are there any messages?"

"Yes, Doctor, Major Waters called; he just said to call him."

Chapter Fourteen

──◆──

Insight Is a Breath Away

As I walk back to the group room, looking forward to being away from phones and Command, I hope for a great session. The hope is always there, but today I really need it, need to feel as if something is making a difference and wanting to know that the help I provide could change the outcome of abuse and violence.

I move into the group room again and Booth looks up. His work is out, and he is rifling through some white homework papers. The rest of the group take their seats.

Without missing a beat, Booth looks around and says, "Man, this homework sucks; I hate going over this again and again. Did you hear that that guy, that patient of yours, might be in the hospital? You know, that guy Smith. Maybe his karma caught up with him." He shoots a look at the corpsman, who turns away smirking.

He starts his check-in, but I stop him abruptly. "What are you talking about? I haven't heard anything; are you sure?"

He just shrugs and begins his check-in. I don't want

to let it go but we were already behind and rumors abound, maybe it wasn't true.

"My name is Jefferson; my wife's name is Annie. I have no kids, one dog. There was lots of alcohol involved. I yelled at my wife, told her I was gonna kill her dog 'cause it was pissing on the carpet. That f'ing mutt just pissed and pissed on that carpet."

The group snickers at the pissing dog. They aren't laughing at Booth, of course, but are with him as he tells his story. Humor aids the healing process at times, but it is odd how much laughing goes on about such frightening and horrific acts of human violence perpetrated on a loved one or the suggested torturing of an animal that is the loved one of a spouse. The laughing continues until I put up my hand.

"Booth, you know that there is a lot more than that, although that is a big piece. DV sometimes does involve the pets, why?"

The group responds, "Power and control, that's why, Doc." None of them believes their response. They just say what I want to hear so they won't get kicked to the curb, their careers ended because they threatened to kill a dog.

Booth begins again, "Okay, okay, I wanted to intimidate her. I wanted to hurt her like she hurt me. I wanted to scare her and make her stay with me and do what I said. I am the man of the house, the one who makes the money."

At the end of the table, Carson is fidgeting constantly. I can see he really feels out of place with these guys.

"How'd that work for you?" I ask Booth.

He answers sincerely, "It didn't, and she made me hurt myself, too."

Goodman speaks up, and everyone applauds. "He's

blaming, isn't he?"

"You're right, Goodman," I respond. "That's a great insight, thanks. Booth, just get back to what got you here."

Booth keeps going, "My wife moved out 'cause of our fighting and my drinking, but before it got physical. She came over to get the dog, and I held it up over her head. It was real little; I was drunk, and I told her she had to jump for it, and that I was going to kill it. She jumped for it and almost got it; I pushed her with one hand; she fell against the screen door. It opened, and she fell down the stairs in front of the house and busted her nose on the cement step. There was blood everywhere; she was yelling; I was yelling, and someone called the police. I was arrested, but it did really start over the dog."

Martinez is visibly upset. "Where is the dog now? You weren't really gonna kill it, were you?"

Booth shows no emotion. "Yeah, I was really gonna kill it. That's one of the big reasons that got me here, is just telling the truth. I really was gonna kill that dog. She always did love that f'ing animal more than me. She treated him better."

Martinez is horrified. "What's wrong with him, Doc? What's the belief behind that?" She isn't in tears; she knows too well not to cry before these fellow marines, but the fear and loathing is easy to see on her face.

Without pause I hand it to Booth, "What do you think?"

"That's the thing. I always saw my parents do shit like that. Where I come from in Georgia, that's just how it is. My dad did that to my mom, and you seen that movie *Affliction*, right? Well, my dad was Nick Nolte: drinking, hitting. He threw our cat through the barn window once, and I thought for sure she was dead, but she wasn't. She just got back up, but she never came near my dad again. None of us tried to get near him."

I want to know if he really got it. "So, what do you think your belief was, Booth?"

"I'm the man, do what I say."

"Or?"

"Or I'll f'ing hurt you. Or I'll hurt what you love until you do what I want."

Finally, he was getting there. "Good! That sounds right on. Anyone else? So, what did you bring in to show what you want instead of what you have?"

Booth sighs. "Well, she's gone, and that's my fault. I did a lot of real bad things to her, and I feel bad about that. I'm lonely, and I do want to get better, go to AA, and what I brought in is a song that speaks to me …" He trails off.

The entire group chimes in at this, with an "Awwwwwwww …"

I hold up my hand. "Stop it; let him go on."

"The song I brought in is 'Sweet Home Alabama.' That song speaks to my heart. It's about home. It's about love. All the things I miss."

Goodman chimes in, "Aren't you from southern Georgia, not Alabama, Booth?"

"Yeah," Booth admits, "but I want that feeling, home sweet home with someone who wants to be with me, love me, and who I can trust and treat real good, not like before, not like it is now. No one. There is another deployment coming up, with no one to care or to wait for me. I just want to go home to some home I've never had, but that's how I want it different."

Carson begins talking before there is any appreciable break in the conversation.

"I'm ready. My name is John; my ex-wife is Michelle; we're both marines. There was alcohol on her part, and …"

But I won't let him continue until he corrects himself. "Don't tell us what she did."

Carson proceeds cautiously, realizing his error. "I took her car keys, so she couldn't drive. I took them from her again (this is weird talking so one-sided). We both have been trained; we started grappling and tussling, trying to put the other one down and get control, and we both fell through the front window of the house onto the lawn in base housing. The MPs were there already on another call and saw us. They arrested us both. We both refused medical attention, even though we were both cut up a bit. This was mutual; it was decided that it was mutual. We both must do this group crap, and if she had just given me those keys I wouldn't be here. But we both must go, and now we are in divorce proceedings." Carson's tempo starts out as slow and methodical but picks up as he clearly is frustrated thinking about the event. "Her Command contacted mine. There is a Military Protective Order, but I know I did the right thing, not letting her drive. So where is the fairness? It's a bunch of bullshit that I'm here."

Carson looks over at Booth, "Were you done, man?"

Booth nods.

Carson looks at Booth, "You better not say it."

I address him directly, "Carson, why are you here?"

"Well, Doc, they said I should never have put my hands on her or used military training to subdue her or control her. I never did get those keys. They said before I touched her I should have left, called the MPs to prevent her from driving, but when I put my hands on her to control her actions, I broke the law. What do you think?"

"Would you do anything differently next time?" I ask him.

Carson seems resigned. "Well, she's gone; we're divorcing, and so there won't be a next time."

"Carson, you're smart; what about another relationship? Would you do it again?"

"No."

"Good. That's progress. What did you bring in?"

"I brought in a banjo my dad left me. He was a sergeant major in the marines, the reason I became a marine. He taught me how to play it. He taught me to play it if I felt bad; he said playing it would help bad feelings pass away, move along until they were gone. When the last note was played the bad feelings would end with the song. He said to look forward instead of back. I would listen to him play for hours, just sit and stare at him. My mom left us when I was five, and he just got so sad after that. The only time I saw him smile is when he played and when we sang some of those real old songs, real hokey songs. So, I brought in the banjo."

"So how does this represent how you want your life and your future relationship to be? How does this represent you now?" I ask him.

"I guess I'm just battered. Forgive the expression, my dad leaving just destroyed me," he says as an afterthought.

Everyone laughs, and the mood lightens a bit. Carson wants to finish, and the group quiets down.

"I am bruised, but this old banjo represents perseverance. Semper f'ing Fi, loyalty, and all that. If I can just keep going, play through it, it's going to be all right. If I can really learn to play it, to embrace it, it might tell me something about myself that will help me be a better person, like my dad. He never hit a woman, even after my mom did what she did to him. He sang; he was there for me; he included me and made me feel safe. I guess that's how I want to see myself, safe, and sharing that with someone I love. So instead of mutually abusive it could be mutually protective.

"I got a lot to learn; I know I'm not one of the f'ing few, the f'ing proud. I was arrogant and prideful, but it's that kind of pride that got me here. My dad was part of the few and the proud that marines look up to and honor. His pride was won in theater as a leader of men and by safeguarding his family. Maybe if I stop fooling myself and take responsibility I can get there. So here it is."

He pulls out the tattered old banjo. It has frayed strings and a worn fret at the top. The body is stained and dirty, and what was originally white is now a tannish orange with age.

Booth speaks up, but not to disrupt. Instead, he appears concerned and sincere. "Man, that was f'ing deep, the few, the proud … yeah, that's f'ing deep. I am gonna think about that."

I look at Goodman. "You said nothing last time; you look really depressed, too. Have you been to the naval hospital yet, seen the psychiatrist?"

"Yeah, I went. I'm taking something, but there's no real treatment. They're kicking me out. I'm just waiting for my court-martial, and I would rather come here. It's the only place I feel safe."

"So, what happened? Did you have another incident?" I ask Goodman as he sits with gloom apparent on his face.

"I know there was an MPO, but I just couldn't stop it. I wanted to see my son, and my wife wouldn't let me. I pay for that house, and I can't even see my son. She's keeping him from me."

Time to start the ritual over again. "So, what is the check-in?"

"I am Ray Goodman; my wife's name is Mamie; my son's name is Ray Goodman Jr. I pushed my wife, strangled my wife until she passed out. I threw her into the glass coffee table, and she got twenty-three stitches in her back. I was arrested, spent four weeks in the brig; my rank was busted down, and there is still an MPO, so I can't go to my house or see my son. That's what got me here. Then I went back, broke into the house for my razor to cut my hair, and was arrested again."

"This police report I just got today said you went to the house again at four a.m. for razor blades. What's that about?"

"I had to shave my head, and I needed a razor."

"You had to have it from your wife's residence, which you are prohibited from entering, at four a.m.? You're not supposed to go near your family. It says here you broke down the door, and your son was screaming so loud the neighbors called the police."

Goodman is wringing his hands while he listens, and as he talks he clenches and opens his hands. Either he is doing the muscle tense and relax techniques for self stress relief or he is feeling very frustrated—probably both.

"I don't remember breaking down the door. I remember hearing him cry, and I remember yelling, 'I want to see my son!' I don't remember anything after that until the holding cell."

I think hard about what to say next. What would move him toward realization and progress? "I still don't understand why you are back here. You will have to have another CRC, you know, military case review committee board, because there is another incident. I am supposed to dismiss you from group."

He looks like I have hit him. "I just want to be here with you; I feel okay here, and my case manager is going to call you. I am being administratively separated from the Marine Corps, court-martialed—everything they can do to me. I probably won't ever get to see my kid or my wife again. I just want to be here. Is that okay with you?" He is almost pleading at this point, but a marine doesn't beg. He feels safe here, open. This isn't the first time a marine felt better here than anywhere else in the world.

Booth shakes his head, "Man, I don't get it. I can't wait to get out of here and get these people out of my life—no disrespect, ma'am—and you just keep coming back here. Man, you are one crazy mo-fu."

I glare at him. "That's enough, Booth."

Goodman wants to keep going, and I relinquish the floor to him. "Here is what I brought in for show and tell."

Goodman holds up a Pat the Bunny book, and Tatum looks over at it with a sour expression. "What the hell is that?"

"It's my son's favorite book; you don't need words to love it. It makes me feel good to hold it and pat it and remember when we were together. I don't have words; I just feel bad all the time, and I see my son's face at night, and I miss him. He never hurt me; he doesn't deserve this, and I want to see him and go through the book together."

I speak up this time. "Goodman, do you see your part in why you are not together with him?"

"I can't remember, I told you. I just know it's Mamie who's told on me every time. It's Mamie; she just wants to ruin my career."

Tatum sighs so everyone can hear. "Man, you ain't

never getting outta here, you idiot. Don't you know you can't say something like that? Even if you think it, you don't say that. You say you did it, and it's not her fault; that's what you say, you idiot."

That's all it takes. Ray breaks down crying, his head in his lap with the bunny book.

We need to clear the air. "We're taking a break. Goodman, you stay with me, and you guys go smoke outside or something. Be back in ten minutes."

They file out, pulling their cigarettes out of their rolled-up sleeves. I take Goodman by the arm to the end of the hallway. "Do you trust me?"

"Yeah."

"Why do you think you keep coming back here even when you don't have to, because you're getting kicked out?"

"I don't know; I just like being in this room with you."

"So, you feel safe with me, right? You know I'm not going to shame you or hurt you, right?"

"Yeah, I guess so."

"What do you think Mamie really wants? How safe do you think she feels? Don't you suppose she wants much of what you want?"

Clearly, Goodman is trying. Therapy is much like the methodology of the service. Before you can build a man up, you must remove all the bullshit, all the ego, all the lies. Goodman sits before me broken, but ready to be fixed. He sits there crying, but ready to heal. I can see it, though it is probably too late to save his career.

"I just don't remember anything after driving up to the house and pounding on the door. It all just went blank until I was in custody. She did look terrified. The police said the neighbors heard me yelling that I was gonna kill her, and my son was screaming, 'Daddy, don't! Daddy don't!' He looked so scared. I just wish I were dead."

"Really? How would you do it, Goodman? Pills, rope?"

"I've got enough Xanax saved from over this last year to do it. I just want to see my son before."

"Before what, Goodman?" I ask, in a low but reassuring voice—not the stern voice I have used all morning with Command, or the understanding but firm voice I use in group.

"Nothing, it doesn't matter; my life means nothing. I've screwed everything up so many times, and I don't have any other chances left. They're kicking me out; I have nowhere to go, and I know I'm not gonna see my son."

The rest of the group are talking uneasily on the corner. They all stand with a cigarette in hand, puffs of smoke pluming out over their heads. As I counsel Goodman I notice corpsman disengage from the group. He stares off to the side at Smith, who is approaching the center from the street.

Corpsman nudges Booth. "You see that guy? That's him. The POG that made out he was a grunt, and he deals too, right?"

"Yeah, I know about that guy. He's gonna get it; he's

gonna get his; karma is a bitch. He gave something to a gunny's girlfriend, and she OD'd, almost wound up dead, and she's still in the hospital. I knew he was a dealer. I hear the gunny's friends are going to really mess him up. Things are getting cleaned up around here." They continue to stare at him. Smith seems nervous, twitching and overanimated. He is saying something to a young woman at the end of the building.

Carson and Martinez are sitting on the steps talking quietly. "I hope you weren't too hard on your daughter for taping over that song you like so much. Were you able to get a tape of it for the group today?"

"No, I calmed down before I saw her. She didn't mean to; she loves that Little Tykes recorder. She's always sneaking up behind me while I'm cooking and recording what I say. Sometimes we pretend we have a cooking show, and she interviews me like I'm a famous chef. Her favorite is the dessert top chef show where I make her favorite angel cookies because her name is Angel. We make little cinnamon wings and tiny halos out of sprinkles ..."

Martinez stands up and turns to Carson. "I didn't find another recording, so I can either play the song up until the place where she recorded over it or wait until I can find the tape or a CD. It's too bad. I'd really like to share it with everyone."

"What's the name again?" Carson asks.

"'I'll Be Home for Christmas.'" They walk back in and Carson puts a light arm on her shoulder.

"I'm going to the Base Exchange (BX) today; I'm gonna find it."

I peer around the corner and say so they can all hear, "Breaks over, come on back."

The group take their seats again. The mood is still low, but lighter and everyone seems more at ease.

"Corpsman, you and Martinez haven't checked in today, but I'm afraid we are going to have to end a bit early. I'm concerned about a group member, and he and I are going to walk over to the hospital together."

Goodman looks up surprised but not shaken, "Really, you really think I need that?"

"Yeah, I really do, and I don't want to call Command to escort you. No drama. You've had enough drama. I'd rather go over with you and make the soft handoff if that's okay with you."

"Yeah, okay ..."

He just sits and stares. I don't know what he is thinking. He knows his career is over, but like all of us, a glimmer of hope may encourage him. In this case he would be administratively separated from the marines; out of the only career he has known. It will be better not to focus on that; he is still probably a danger to himself.

The corpsman speaks up and offers his hand. "I have to go over there anyway to pick up some paperwork, I can give you a ride. It's at least a mile to walk."

It's a nice offer, but I don't want to take it. "Thanks, but I could use the walk, and I think it's better to walk with Goodman than put him in a car right now."

"Oh yeah, I get you." He knows I am concerned.

Goodman might try to jump from a car if his feelings overwhelmed him. "I'll walk with you, too, then."

"Thanks, man." Goodman could use the company.

I can't forget to give homework to the group. It is the little things that bridge sessions, keep people thinking about the group dynamic, and maintain a positive movement toward health.

"Do the regular homework for next week. Martinez, bring your symbol of what you want, and you, too, corpsman, next time."

"What do you want *me* to do?" Goodman asks. I know he won't be back.

I smile. "For right now just walk with me and see yourself getting better, living past this. I'll stay with you today and make sure you get settled. Your son does need a dad, and I want you to stay in the moment; don't think too far forward or too far in the past. Just stay with me in the moment. Let's go. See everyone next group."

Everyone walks out, and there is Smith waiting for his appointment. I step aside for a quick second to talk with Smith briefly. I tell him I heard he was in the hospital. He doesn't know what I am talking about and looks disappointed, but I have to leave with Goodman and corpsman, who are already on the way out of the building.

The corpsman turns to Smith and says under his breath, "Karma is a bitch, man. Remember that."

Smith wipes his nose and appears to not understand him. I don't know what this is about, but Smith is clearly confused and alarmed.

"Who are you? What are you talking about?" Smith whimpers. But the corpsman has already passed by, with me and Goodman. We walk down the street, Goodman between corpsman and me, maybe three feet between us. My phone buzzes with the sound of a swarm of mosquitoes. I put it to my ear.

It's Sam. "Hey you, I was just thinking about you. I'm walking over to the hospital. It's a beautiful day, and a couple of friends of mine and I are heading over to the mental health unit. What are you up to?"

Sam speaks up confidently, "You were right. How does that feel? Miller was not suicidal; it's now officially a homicide. I don't want to say too much over the phone; can we meet later? What about Del Mar beach about five? Don't you like to go down there and walk some days after work?"

"That sounds wonderful. I could use the exercise, and it also calms me down. I'll see you there. If I'm going to be late, I'll leave you a message."

After a twenty-minute walk we arrive at the hospital. Medical technicians in white lab coats start brushing by feverishly, and two come out to meet us. The handoff process is simple. The office called ahead, and the mental health unit techs are out front to meet us. Goodman bends down and hugs me; then walks through the double doors, which are unlocked with magnetic keys. I can see him looking back toward me sadly. As the doors close, so does his career. He won't be coming back into duty after this latest incident. There is nothing more I can do for him. He'll be released, and his life will have to begin anew. I can only hope he finds the solace that we all deserve. Will it be today for me? No, I suppose not.

A feeling of relief that I have helped Goodman to protect himself, but probably ended his career at the same time, washes over me. There is nothing else I could have done to help, I know, but here was a young warrior who had sworn his life and lost his family. I intended differently for him.

I turn to corpsman. "That was really nice of you to walk with us. You didn't have to do that. You're a complex person. Sometimes you seem so caring, open, kind—the essence of a healer. I can see at those times why people really come to you for help; I could really see that happening in a war zone. I feel your confidence. But other times you just seem so bitter, like you're going to really hurt someone, even someone you care about like your wife. What's the deal?"

The corpsman stands silent for a second, and then looks directly at my face—something people rarely do in group. "Well, I guess I'm just an enigma, Doc. Maybe I'm the one guy you just can't figure out, huh?"

"Oh. I never want you to think I'm trying to figure you out." I pause and then laugh. "It's funny you say that. I get that a lot; people think I know what they're thinking, or I care what they're thinking. I'm not trying to do that at all. If you show up and want help, if you want to make yourself vulnerable, look within to find your own answers, I'm available. Creating a safe environment is what it's about, what I'm about. I accept people where they are. I try not to judge. I guess it's how I'd want to be treated."

The corpsman looks away. "You're a good person, Doc, and I actually think you mean that, but I think some people who really hurt other people don't get better by just talking about it." He pauses.

"They use words to connive, to manipulate, just to get what they want no matter how it hurts people or takes things away from other people. Those people need something different. They're too bad, too evil to be helped. War doesn't make them. They're just like that."

My phone rings again, and I must answer. "We'll continue this later, corpsman; I have to go."

It's Sam's ringtone, and I immediately answer, "Hey, I'm leaving now; I'll meet you on the beach down by the egret preserve. I can catch a ride on the hospital shuttle and be there in about ten minutes."

Chapter Fifteen

———◆———

Love Speaks Softly

Outside, I hail a government van that is just about to leave the parking lot. The door opens, and I hop in. The van winds down the road across the freeway, past the barracks and the sign that marks Del Mar Beach. I jump out and walk past the lifeguard stands, all the way along the beach to the bird nesting grounds. I sit on the damp sand and look out at the surf, the seagulls skimming the water, and the sun just about to set. The sky is glowing red, and the sound of the surf is strong as it pushes up onto the beach about a yard from me.

Natural life—surroundings quite different from the sterile and unnatural lighting of my office. The smells are cool and crisp here, salty but not overwhelming, and the feeling that I belong here and not in my office is strong. This is my therapy, my escape, my relaxation, and my moment of bliss. If I could be anywhere it would be here. Figures jog by me; marines enjoying the afternoon sunlight and the respite that only nature can give them.

Sam approaches, and I wave. As he moves closer he calls out, "Hey, hey, isn't this beautiful?" The sound of the waves is deafening. He is still shouting as he gets closer, and there is no one else on this patch of beach. He jogs up out of breath.

"So why were you at the hospital?" he asks, panting.

I give him a hug as he recovers. "I had someone in my group that I felt could really harm himself, so instead of having his Command just grab him and take him to the mental health unit—I know this guy; he might have resisted and gotten hurt—I thought it was better just to walk him over myself. It seemed more humane."

"That's why I love you."

I look at him, rather shocked. There is a beat, a pause before Sam recovers. Speaking rapidly, but low, he explains, "That's what I love about you; you really care; you see family violence all the time; you see these guys crazy as bats coming back from deployments, and you still care; you still see past the craziness to care about helping them. But I don't know, I think sometimes these people just need something else."

It is time to talk about what's on my mind, and I know I can trust him. "Sam, I have wanted to talk to you about that guy who killed all of those people at Fort Hood. Do you know about that case? That guy was a trained psychiatrist; he turned on those other caregivers and killed them. I just don't get it. Was it that he just couldn't take it, that the suffering just got to him? Or was it a terrorist thing, religious zealotry ... what was it? I need to know."

Sam takes my hands and holds them to rub them together and keep them warm. He is so loving and gentle, a sharp contrast to the job he does on the base. "I don't know for sure, but I know they have intel that he was involved with a cleric who was a terrorist. He was speaking threats that people didn't listen to, but I think he did see the worst PTSD cases, and he was broken by them. I don't know where you draw the line, or where we say, 'I'm out of here; I can't take this.' Of course, he was a major and didn't have the option to just quit like you can, Miss Civilian."

"I hear about something like this, and I don't know, I think there's always hope, and the day that I don't, that's the day I'm gonna just leave and do something else. I guess I'm different. I'm a civilian in an uncivil environment. It's tough, every day it's tough ..." I know my voice is trailing off, but I can't help it. I feel like crying more than ever.

With that, Sam sits down next to me on the beach and puts his arm around me. I can hear his voice in my ear. "What would you do, if you left? What new adventure would you be up to?"

"I don't know. I figured when Blake left, maybe I would go teach abroad or even, like he said, do a tour in Iraq or Afghanistan as an embedded counselor. I think I might be of use. But if it's just for me, maybe go look for the Loch Ness monster like my dad did in his yawl when he retired from the service. You know, just tour through the lochs, get a little cold, drink some tea, and see what I could find." I smile with those thoughts. Those dreams seem so far away sometimes.

"Well, I have the boat. It's not a yawl but it's seaworthy and ready to go. I just sailed it up the coast to Maine last summer. You should sail with me. Could you see yourself sailing with me?"

I lean over and kiss him, stroke his head.

"I would love to sail with you. I need to get Blake off to the rest of his life, you know, college, and stay close for a while to reassure him, and then I'll be ready. What are your plans for the next few years? You love NCIS, don't you? What about making your climb up the chain of Command; I thought you wanted that?"

"I don't know, since we've met I think of things differently. I think of you and how things fit around you. I know I never had kids, and even if yours is a young man now, and your daughter is almost grown, I have a lot to learn about how to relate to them. But I want to learn; you always say that's the difference, isn't it? Come on, I'll take you back to the office. You do so much; I just want to be the one that takes care of you a little bit."

I hug him as we walk toward the parking lot.

Sam continues talking to me as I enjoy the moment. "I wanted to meet you to tell you about what the ME found. Miller was injected with something, probably a stimulant like epinephrine. He didn't hang himself at all; he was dead when he was put in that position. It had to be done by someone else, and at least two people. You were right; he wasn't suicidal, and there were no civilians signed into that area at the time of death. It had to be earlier than we thought. We think there might be a link between this and some other injuries to rogue marines."

Chapter Sixteen

———◆———

One Voice Silenced, Another Found

I'm driving into work the following day, when I see a black SUV behind me in traffic. I recognize the car, but I can't recall when and where I've seen it. I have that anxious feeling you get as you're being watched, but I try to ignore it. It's a gnawing sensation at the back of your skull—not a premonition, but not something I could simply wave off. I adjust my mirror and see one of Miller's roommates in the vehicle. His shaven head and hardened features are hard to forget. I'm not quite sure what to make of it, if anything, but I keep driving forward. The roommate moves on, but not before we lock eyes. He knows he has been recognized; I am sure of it, and he moves faster and farther away. I think about what Sam had said about a vigilante group in the military and I wonder if that is possible.

As I pull in, the clock strikes eight, and I see all the cars that were previously moving in both directions now stopped along the road. I barely squeak by into the parking lot as the flag is hoisted onto the pole, and the service members stand at attention on the street saluting. It's another marine ritual that never ceases to impress me. Where else would drivers pull over, stop, get out of their cars, and salute the country that gives them freedom and liberty? The "Star-Spangled Banner" plays as I get out of my car and stand next to it. The music ends, and the cars resume driving.

I fumble with my keys for a second, and then unlock the counseling center door. From my office I can hear the group members begin to file in to the counseling services building. They check in at the desk and sit down; they must always check in and wait to be called into the group room. That is protocol. Fox News is on and the war dead are saluted as the scroll rolls by. I hear the secretary quickly change stations to a sports channel. Sports channels are always safe, and she has been told never to allow any war-related news on the TV, especially casualty statistics.

I am just coming out of my office when sirens begin to wail. MP cars speed past—one, two, three cars. The large plate-glass windows on the counseling center building rattle as they drive by. The men waiting for group are now on their feet, some running outside and looking toward the Serra Mesa housing area, east of the building.

Booth comes by them on his way into the building. I hear him tell the rest of the group to come inside; they follow him in. "Man, something is going on in Serra Mesa housing development! Every PMO car is down there, and I just saw an ambulance almost flying past. What's going down?" They are all standing in the building entryway. He asks the secretary, "Doesn't your husband work over at PMO? Call him and ask him what the hell is going on."

She picks up the phone and speaks briefly to someone. She looks grim, transfixed, as she hangs up the phone and plops down in her chair, looking shocked and stunned.

Booth drawls, "What? What? What's the matter with you? I know you haven't worked here very long, but you gotta talk to the customers, ma'am; it's part of your job."

She gets up crying and runs down the hall to me, where I am standing in the doorway of my office. I could hear part of the conversation from the reception area before and the commotion outside, but I had hoped not to be drawn in.

"What is it?" I ask. "What the ..." I open the door wider to let her in, and the secretary, crying, collapses on the large chair next to where I sit at my desk. I move faster than I had thought possible to shield her from onlookers. I slam the door shut and sit down at my desk.

"What is it? What's wrong? Did someone say something to you? Were those guys mean or rude to you? I'm just about to do group; I'll confront them with it and have them apologize to you. I'm really sorry; the things you hear and see here are just ..."

"Stop. Stop it. I know you mean well but it's not that. Someone is dead in Serra Mesa. My husband said for me not to go home; we live down there. He said there's blood all over at one unit; he doesn't want me to see it. I have never heard of stuff like this where we were stationed before. I don't think I can work here; that's right down the street from us ... that could have been me ... my family ..." She is sobbing now in the chair.

I tell the secretary to stay in my office, and I hurry out to the front, past the group members who are still in the building, either wanting to avoid more stress or uninterested in the terror outside. More cars whiz by, and people are gathering up the street at the entrance to the housing area. There is a barricade there now, and people are being held back.

The counseling manager motions me back in.

Looking into the distance, not at me, the manager relays her message, "Fox, come back here. I just got a call from the provost marshal, and he said to get people into the building who belong in here. There is an investigation ongoing; they need things brought under control. Start group now, please."

My interests are up the street, but it's the right move. I call to the group, "Come on in here, guys; we need to get started." I go in and sit at the table. They won't want to start in this commotion, and it will be hard to get any focus at all, but it must happen.

The group members move slowly and reluctantly toward the counseling room. The corpsman is first. "I'm here; I have my homework and my little something extra," he calls out to the nearly empty room. It's just he and I at this point. He pauses, looking around. "Where is everyone?" he asks, suspiciously.

I smile. "You're the first one here. You know, corpsman, I was thinking about our discussion. People can get better, emotionally and psychologically. They can survive addiction and abuse; I see it happening. It isn't pretty what they go through looking at their dark side, but there is a path to the light."

"I know, I'm a healer. Why are you telling me this?" He seems irritated. Either he has forgotten our discussion the day before, or he is just being defensive.

"It was something you said when we were taking Goodman over to the hospital, something you said to my patient last week who was waiting outside the door."

"What are you talking about? I have no idea what you mean." He is a bit ruffled, but not angry.

"You didn't think I heard you tell him 'Karma is a bitch?'"

"Oh yeah, that. I just think what goes around comes around."

"So, if you are a healer, and you know someone is about to harm another person, even if that person is wretched, are you any better than the person who beats them up if you don't stop it? I am talking about Smith. He almost died; someone jumped him yesterday, and he's still in ICU. You and Booth were talking about that in group before it happened. I just got a call, he was beaten almost to death, and you guys knew about this, didn't you? Are you better than the scum ball you want physically punished? Who decides who the right and just ones are?"

"A lot of people hated that guy; he almost killed someone by giving them drugs." The corpsman is being honest. I can see it in him. He is angry, or irritated, or afraid. The corpsman believes what he is saying and isn't afraid to show it.

I go on, "He survived, you know. He got beaten up badly, but he survived. Maybe he has a chance, or maybe you're right—he'll just get out and do it all over again. But what part do we each play in that, and how does our conscience come to terms with our dark side? I feel pretty clean; how do you feel?"

The corpsman is thinking about it, but his face shows frustration, perhaps guilt. I'm not sure exactly what he is feeling, but I know I have hit a chord.

After a long moment, Tatum enters the room with the traditional greeting. "OO-rah!" he calls out in a cheery voice.

Irritated, the corpsman says, "Why the hell are you so excited, man? It's just group again."

Tatum replies, "Hey, I had barbeque last night! I had my last EMDR session last week, and I ate barbeque last night! Shawna and I had sex afterward, too. OO-rah, OO-rah, OO-rah! It's a damn good life."

"I don't want to hear about your sex life, Tatum." Corpsman sneers. Carson comes in and looks around for an open seat.

"Hey all ..." He pauses. "Where's Martinez?"

Booth is right behind him. "She's probably just running late. There's a huge barricade down the street; I could hardly get around the corner near Serra Mesa. There's a swarm of MPs over there."

I know nothing will get done here unless some answers to the commotion down the street are sought, so I start to leave the room to ask a question or two. At least this will satisfy the curiosity that would otherwise fester in the group all morning.

"Let me see what's going on," I say.

Just as I exit the room, the manager approaches and orders me back inside. I think about that—she is ordering me. A civilian, out of the chain of command, is being ordered by another civilian to do something. I wasn't being asked. It wasn't being recommended to me. This day in day out working in the military environment has almost broken my spirit, but not quite. I have always been a free spirit, someone who doesn't take orders, and here this person is ordering me to do something against my judgment.

In this second, I know my moment has come. I can either back down and sit meekly in this room, or I can find my voice, disregard her blatant command, and show that I am more than just an employee for the federal government to order around.

I stand in the doorway of the group counseling room staring at the counseling manager. My thoughts race. The unnatural light, fluorescent orange glowing on green carpeting that mimics grass, makes me think of the major who went postal at Fort Hood. I see the manager's expectation that her order will be followed immediately. Do I acquiesce—do what she says and kowtow as usual, or do I finally speak up, be the professional person I always was before I came to this soul-killing place? I stand there for what seems like an eternity, staring at the manager. If I tell her no, there will be consequences. But if I don't stop her from running over me now, it will be the final muffling of my existential scream.

With new conviction, I smile and in a light tone, I say, "No."

She recoils back in disbelief.

Carson comes out of the room right behind me and breaks the tension, only to add more with his words. "Something's wrong; I can feel it. Something's happened to her. When did she say her old man was getting out?"

Booth seems concerned as well but tries to offer comfort. "Man, I don't know. I can't remember. Carson, just chill, what's wrong with you? She's probably just late, that's all. Maybe her daughter had some problem. All my friends with kids run late—can't find a show, have to change their pants ... I'm sure she's fine."

Carson turns on him and yells, "Shut up, Booth!"

I return to the room and shut the door on the flabbergasted manager. Carson is visibly upset. The others seem to be trying to talk to each other, but he brushes them off or ignores them. We can hear the police radios outside the windows, and the military police have cordoned off the street.

"There sure is a lot of chatter on the radio," I begin, "but I can't tell what's going on. Booth is right though. There is something going on at Serra Mesa. We need to wait to hear the facts. We have a choice either to get started, or if you need to go find out, you can go without being penalized for missing a group. I am making that decision regardless of what the rules of the program are."

Booth answers quickly, "I want to stay and do my work in here; I want to get it done. I can finally say that she didn't do nothing to provoke me; she doesn't have to forgive me. 'Course we're divorced now, and she won't talk to me, so that ain't a problem." Booth laughs with the final irony that sometimes forgiveness isn't a problem. The new people in the group look uncomfortable. Carson is still looking out the window and seems very nervous.

"I know she was coming; I got her that tape. I even found the f'ing tape, not even a CD, so she could play it with her daughter. And bring it here on that stupid Little Tykes player she uses. Why she doesn't just get that f'ing stereo fixed, I don't know. I'm gonna fix that for her." He starts mumbling; he is breaking down. His voice trails off while he still looks out the window. We need to start; Carson needs to focus in, that will get his mind off Martinez.

"You new guys, you think you shouldn't be here; somebody lied, and it wasn't your fault ..."

Carson snaps back into the conversation suddenly and with severe irritation demands, "Do you really have to go over that again?"

I sigh. This isn't the first time the question will be asked, and it won't be the last. "I did it for you when you were new; I do it for them, the newbies. You see how it's the same, Carson, how offenders always think of themselves as the victims of injustice at first? No matter what they did, no matter what their story is, you see it will be the same, the same denial, the same blaming the real victim. People don't realize in the heat of arguments and innuendo that feelings aren't facts; they let perceptions blinded by old beliefs send them down a pathway that leads to violence, and they keep doing it, the same minimizing until they finally look at their dark side, at the beliefs that justified hurting their 'loved one.'"

It's a painful, distorted, and self-absorbing, self-defeating loop that plays over and over like a repeating tape, I think. Carson keeps looking around; he's anxious and nervous, and he's not paying attention to anything going on in group. I take pity on him. "Carson, you can go if you need to; go check; you won't be counted as missing group."

I turn back to the others. "If you guys would just stop hurting those you love, we could end the group—last guy or gal denial, last act of blaming. But it goes on and on and on; some get it; some get it a little and can at least have a nonviolent relationship if they don't get to a mutually satisfying partnership. But at least they won't be back here. And then there are those like Sergeant Houser here." I look at one of the new guys; so does the rest of the group. I sigh. Sergeant Houser doesn't understand, but he has had the right answers before.

"Haven't we been through this a couple of cycles, sergeant?" He scowls at me. He hates me; I can see it in his eyes. I can see the contempt, the blaming.

"I thought so. Well, maybe the dear sergeant here will never get it, but we won't give up. We never give up." I smile and look around the room.

Carson gets up and bolts out the door. He yells behind him, "I got to go see. I know something is wrong. Just mark me absent; tell my Command; I don't care."

Everyone moves to the window and watches Carson dash through the police lines and up the street. We see him run all the way up to Serra Mesa housing. The military police are everywhere, and barricades are being put in place. The group watches in stunned silence. I know I must go, too. I move quickly to leave the building. The manager catches me by the arm on the way out, and in her most parental tone tells me I must go back and finish group.

Again, my message is unmistakable: "No," I tell her plainly. She stumbles back and falls to the floor without a push. She is literally bowled over in disbelief at my newfound voice.

Carson has quite a lead on me. I can see an MP block his way as he gets close to the center of the action. I am stopped by a CID agent halfway up the street. He wants to know why I am running up to Serra Mesa housing. Do I know something? The interchange seems to take forever. I don't want to disrespect the agent, but I don't want to lose track of Carson, whom I can now barely see through the gathering crowd. A military policeman is talking to him and I hear Carson respond, "My CO sent me to check on his marine."

The MP lets him through. I get away from the CID agent and make it to the barrier, but I have no business to declare that will let me pass. Carson is up near a house where broken glass is strewn across the lawn and smoke is pouring from the windows. I can only act as a voyeur to his journey now.

The front door of the burning house is hanging off its hinges; the smells coming from inside are of smoke and something foul and dead. The medics are taking a body out with a white sheet over it. I can hear Carson frantically yelling at the medic: "Male or female?"

No one answers.

"Male or f'ing female?"

The medic looks up without interest. *"Female. Female."* Carson pushes closer and stops the medic. He raises the sheet and gags as he bursts into tears. They leave with the body. Carson tries to rush into the house, but an MP places his hand on the distraught marine's chest, barring his way. He looks directly in Carson's eyes.

"This is a crime scene; nobody can come in here, nobody. The animal that did this got away; we must get everything. The neighbors saw her husband run away; they have her daughter, that poor little thing. She must have seen everything—scarred for life after that. Her mother didn't have a chance, looking at the size of that knife he used. It's all in there, but you can't go in. Are you a friend or from her Command?"

Carson wipes the tears away from his face. He notices Angel's recorder thrown over to the side. There is blood on the bottom of the toy. He is still crying, but with resolve he replies, *"I'm a friend, but I need to get that Little Tykes player to take to Angel, her daughter. It'll calm her down; she needs anything that can help now."*

"Well, I don't know ..."

"I don't see how that can be a part of the investigation, officer. Can I just take it to her?" He points to the player sitting on the lawn.

The MP gives in, *"Okay, just take it. But get out of here. There's blood everywhere; we have lots to do here."*

The MP hands the Little Tykes recorder to Carson.

I see him take the player and round the building to the alley behind. I walk to the far edge of the barrier so I don't lose sight of him. He is studying the player as he moves down the alley behind the house and sits down next to the wall of an adjacent housing unit. He is holding his stomach as if in pain and he looks ill. I call to him, but the crowd is so loud my beckoning is drowned out. I can see him double over, and tears are dripping down his cheeks. I want to go to him, but I am rebuffed by the MP.

Carson pushes the play button and the song begins. I can barely hear a familiar refrain, "I'll be home for Christmas ..." It plays a few words, and then the music suddenly stops and gives way to voices shouting. An angry man's voice is heard, then a woman's, and a child's voice pleading, "Stop, Daddy! Please stop!" It's all there; it rolls on—screaming, crying, stabbing, all captured on that Little Tykes recorder. He sits like a stone, staring and frozen. He hears everything. He hears her die. He hears Angel crying. Carson slumps against the building, sobbing against the brick.

The military policeman who has just spoken with Carson hears the tape playing and leaps round the corner. We have all heard. The noisy crowd is now still and quiet. The MP bends down next to Carson, "Hey, man, give me that f'ing recorder. I knew you shouldn't have taken that; give it to me."

Carson is motionless. He doesn't resist the MP taking the player from his limp hand. The policeman runs off with it, shouting to his sergeant. A group of military police gather around the first MP, listening and motioning. They bag the recorder and remove it. The military policeman walks back to Carson.

"Get up, man. I just got told to tell you to get the hell out of here or get arrested. We know that it's not you on the tape; we have witnesses that saw the guy leaving after the screaming, and it ain't you. My boss is cutting you a break, but he might need to talk to you later. Just get out of here, and for God's sake, suck it up and get yourself together—get ahold of yourself."

Carson struggles up and stumbles slowly out of the crime scene. I am waiting for him at the barricade, where people are still trying to find out what is going on. I reach to put my arm around him and lead him back to counseling services. He walks like a zombie to the counseling building. We walk in together, past the secretary, who tries to ask him questions as we go by, back through the group room door that was left open when we ran out just ten minutes ago. Carson is mumbling aloud, "It was her Someday; it was her dream for Angel ..." His voice cracks; tears stream down his face. "It was Martinez; she should have never been in this f'ing group. She was the victim, not the offender. She never did anything to be here; she was a good person, a loving person. That f'ing guy has gotten away with it before, and now he is just f'ing out there ..."

"Sit down, Carson. What are you talking about?" The others prod him for answers.

Carson waves his hand, bloodied by touching the recorder. "Martinez, the sirens out there; it's Martinez; she's dead; she's dead ..." He cries even harder. He glares at me. "You did nothing to stop it! The f'ing Marine Corps should've stopped him." He moves closer to me, agitated and screaming, getting right in my face with uncontrolled grief. The horrors he has seen all come back to him in this moment of rage and sadness.

Corpsman gets in between us. "Stop it, Carson; get away from her; get out of her face, or we'll all jack you up, man. Back off, I said." Everyone is standing up now, corpsman between Carson and me, corpsman pushing Carson back, Booth grabbing his arms and restraining Carson.

Booth starts talking. It isn't long, or angry, but stern in the way marines talk to each other. "Doc didn't do this to her; her asshole husband did it. The Marine Corps didn't do it to her; she stayed with that guy; she chose to stay. It's awful; it's wrong, but it's not Fox's fault. She tried to help all of us."

Stunned and afraid, I am now against the wall by the large conference room table. I stretch out my arm and fumble for the button underneath. I push it, and I see out of the corner of my eye a blue light begin to flash at the edge of the building. I have tripped the panic button, and the alarm is activated. Booth, Carson, and corpsman are still grappling. Suddenly, the door bursts open and six burly MPs rush in with guns drawn.

"Stop! Everyone, back up. Everyone down, down on the ground, everyone down, hands on the back of your head, straight down, NOW, NOW!!"

Everyone hits the ground. I drop too but am stopped by one of the MPs. He grabs my arm and shakes his head at me, then gently leads me out of the room. "Sergeant Stone, PMO," he introduces himself.

"Sergeant, it's Carson, but don't arrest him." I plead. "He wasn't going to hurt me; he just found out his friend was murdered. He needs intervention. I just wanted him to stop—please don't arrest him!"

Two MPs lead Carson out handcuffed behind his back, followed by Booth and the others. The MP puts Carson in a car, and shouts, "Mental health unit, they're waiting for him!" He raps the top of the vehicle, and it speeds away.

Sergeant Stone looks back at me. "Ma'am, are you all right? Could you come in here, please?" He motions to an adjacent counseling office. As I head there, I see Sam come through the front door. I catch his eye, but no words are exchanged. Another MP, the largest one, emerges from the group room leading corpsman out handcuffed. I get a glimpse of Sam and the MP walking him out and leaving. I am in the room alone now with Sergeant Stone. He hands me some water.

"Ma'am, Agent Waters asked me to remove you from the situation. I can't tell you anything, ma'am. I'm sorry, but you are safe now, and that's my order, keep you safe. I will check to make sure that the building is secured and be back. I will leave one of my men to escort you back to your office, and Agent Waters said he would debrief you later. Thank you for your cooperation, ma'am."

He drops his formal demeanor. "Ma'am, I don't care what they say about you people over here at counseling services, I knew a guy that you really helped, one of my men. I probably won't get the opportunity to tell you again, so I just want to thank you, ma'am; it would not be something I would do, but he got better coming to see you …" He is walking out, but he seems to want to say one more thing. He hesitates.

I motion for him to say whatever it is.

He speaks up, "People ask me all the time how I can

do what I do, see what I see. But I have to ask, how do you do what *you* do, without it getting to you?"

I shrug. I could go into my past, my training, my education. The truth is, I don't know …

He nods in understanding, "Anyways, thanks." He leaves, and the MP comes in, and I am escorted back to my office. I sit down, take some deep breaths, and plug in my smart card to bring up my e-mail. As I look through my messages, a wave of emotion and self-reflection washes over me. Again, the thought, again the pensive question— today, is this The Day that I am so affected by this work, by the mismanagement, that I walk away? I glance over the e-mail, and there is a message from Dr. Streeter.

Patient Goodman has entered a residential program treating dual diagnosis issues. Command is considering not administratively separating him and rehabbing him instead. If he does pull through, he owes it to you. I think today was the day that you saved a service member's life, maybe even his career. I heard you walked the kid over to the hospital. Dedication like that is rare; your service is important; don't give up the good fight. V/R Dale Streeter.

I had intended to sit down and write my resignation, but after reading this e-mail, I hesitate. I need rest. I need to take my own advice. Perhaps this is the day for intervention, not resignation. I fall back into my chair, stare out the window. Nothing is there—so quiet, no hint of emergency, death, domestic violence, or people in crisis. My phone rings.

Sam is there. "Doc, is that you? Are you there?" Just silence from me for a moment.

"Yeah, I'm sorry, I'm just fried. That was unbelievable. Where are you? I was scared this time, Sam. I'm never scared, but this time I was scared."

"I'm here at the brig, with that corpsman. He did it, Fox."

"Did what? What are you talking about? He was trying to help me; he was just restraining Carson. He wasn't attacking me; he was trying to help me."

"I'm not talking about your group. That young woman's death, they're still looking for that woman's husband; they'll get him. That was tragic. They took Carson to mental Health; he's being medicated and treated."

Sam sighs loudly into the phone, "I'm talking about Miller, Sergeant Miller. That corpsman who was helping you, he's the one behind Miller's death, the deliberate killing of Miller. He had a vigilante group that was like some undercover pseudo-operations group that attacked anyone they thought was a threat to the Marine Corps. Smith, he got it from them, too. They would watch who comes to counseling services, who attends groups, and they would pick people they thought should be eliminated from the Marine Corps. Bad seeds gotten rid of. They've been doing this for quite some time. We linked them through counseling services and the base medical, where corpsman had access to the epinephrine that caused Miller's death.

"Are you there? Listen, I'm going to finish up here. He is coming clean and turning in everyone who was involved. It's weird. They have a whole code of ethics that justifies what they did; they think they were helping the Marine Corps. I'm going to leave in a few minutes. I'll come by and follow you home. I'm sure they'll let you off for the rest of the day; they can take over for you for a while. I'll be there soon.

"But you know one of the most tragic things of all about Miller, Doc?"

I just sit in silence and finally manage a response. "What?"

"Miller never took any money. He just told his wife crap to get her to come back to him, and those rumors grew up around that. He literally got killed by rumors. The son of a bitch just died alone, broke and for nothing, just making up stories to seem better off than he was. We found his little carrier bag, and it had nothing in it. And we found verification in Iraq. The guy just did his job like a good marine would. Are you there, Doc?"

Again, there is silence on my end. And then I speak, slowly, and with a low deliberate cadence. "You know, I've really been thinking about that major at Fort Hood, Sam. I realized there is overwhelming evidence he was tied to that radical cleric, and that he did have a terrorist motive. I guess when I thought he was motivated, tortured, and reacting to the exposure he had had to horrific events and human suffering … I guess I was talking about a part of me that just feels dead from the exposure, from not really being able to stem the overwhelming tide of human suffering, only I've just internalized it. I guess I'm hurting more than I imagined. I'm burning out; your shooting star is burning out, Sam. I want to go sailing; I don't know for how long or how far, but I want to take a break. Will you take a break with me, Sam?" As we talk, I see Sam's car roll up outside. I take my things and walk out. The old Porsche looks mighty good to me today. I am happy to be leaving and feel assured with Sam following behind me.

As I turn onto the long winding road that leads from the Marine Base through the Naval Weapons Station and into Fallbrook, I can't get the picture of Carson's bloodied hand out of my head. It's weird how certain images persist. They may not be the most violent images, but they stay with you, in your head, like the members in group. Today was not a good day. I laugh out loud at the absurdity of that self-talk statement. Not a good day. I laugh again. My relaxation CD plays on, and I drive up to the gate that exits the Marine Base and is the gateway to the Naval Weapons Station. The navy guard motions to me to pull over to the search area.

"Crap," I say out loud. Sam is right behind me, and he pulls over, too. This happens so often. I am leaving in the middle of the day, and these guys have nothing better to do. They pick random cars to search completely: everything out of trunks, looking at engines, etc. Even though they saw me this morning, it doesn't matter; they are going to use their time well. Their jobs are incredibly important and stopping an unknown vehicle for a random search is vital to the protection of the base. And even though they recognize my car, it's going to be my turn again.

I watch as Sam gets out of his car, pulls out his ID, and begins a dialogue with the guard. I can't tell what he is saying. I have shown my ID to the guard, so he knows I am a DOD employee. Sam's face is stern, and his posture is a bit puffed up as he speaks.

As they talk, my mind wanders back to what just happened. One of my group members is dead; Carson is at the mental health unit now, and he was the least crazy one of all. He was right that Martinez should not have been in that offender group. She was a victim. Being in the group didn't cause her death, but did the corps get it right with her? The case review committee that recommended she go into an offender group based it on the regulations: she threw something at him, opened his head, and sent him to the hospital. They had no choice but to report it as domestic violence, and Martinez was the offender. DV is messy; it's violent, and everyone loses, especially someone who stays in a violent relationship.

I think about her little girl who has no one now. Her dad will be in prison, and odds are that the three-year-old will be sent to the grandmother, who continues to stay in a loveless marriage of infidelity. Martinez talked so much about her mother's lack of self-esteem and feelings of paralysis in staying. That was the example Corporal Martinez grew up with, and now that is the example her daughter Angel will grow up with. She might very well choose the same type of relationships that other women in that family have chosen. Growing up, that little girl's beliefs about what she deserves, her self-worth, is going to be based on what she learns from what she sees.

My head is leaning on the side of my window when Sam comes up and knocks on it. I put the window down; he can probably see the strain on my face.

"Go ahead; let's go. I don't have a lot of influence, but I can get you through the damn gate."

"Thanks, Sam." We drive on. Without the hassle of the morning commute it's easier to pay attention to the surroundings. There are a hundred Guernsey cows grazing peacefully on the grass that covers the ordnance below. If those cows knew what they were standing on they would amoozed. I laugh; I am really trying to cope now. Off in the distance I can see smoke rising, and a boom reaches my ears. The practicing for war never ends; the drumbeat continues. I realize how small my part seems in this epic drama.

I look back in the mirror, and Sam waves at me. He motions his hand as if patting downward. I know what that means; he thinks I am driving too fast. The consequences can be steep, even revoking the right to travel across the weapon's sacred transitional space. I take heed and slow down. He is really looking out for me. I have never had that before.

As I think about Martinez and her daughter, I can't escape self-examination. I am a colonel's daughter, never coddled; my mother stayed with my cheating father and sucked it up. She didn't leave, and it wasn't until he was deployed and met a civilian employee half his age that my parents got divorced. Even then, the divorce wasn't my mother's bidding. Of course, I have been in therapy for years sorting that out, and I have sought guidance from pastors and spiritual teachers along the way.

I seek self-actualization; God's presence. This passage in my life has given me cause for deep reflection, prayer, and meditation. The extreme violence in working with DV trauma in the military has taken a toll. The abusive and subordinating treatment of clinicians by counseling services management has hurt more. I realize I can't deal with it by myself. My faith is growing in importance to me and looking within is key. How is this really affecting me? How does it affect my relationships—with Sam, with my children? With God? The domestic violence manager, the offenders and victims, the sexual assaults that happen to both men and women, and the traumatized wounded warriors and their families, all contribute to my worldview and my spiritual view.

As I approach the outward gate, I slow to fifteen miles an hour. I get through the gate and back to the civilian world. I am leaving the residue of the base as far behind as I can. This day is finished, and I am done. This is the day.

Martinez's voice is silenced, my voice is found, my spirit is awakened.

About the Author

As a clinician, educator, filmmaker, and writer, Sally Wolf, PhD creates stories that feel deeply personal to the reader, spark insight into the human condition, and illuminate the potential in each of us to change. Through her engaging true-to-life experiences within military and civilian cultures, we are entertained by the mysteries, educated by secrets never shared, and feel inspired to speak our truth. Dr. Wolf gives voice to those who can't speak for themselves and entreats us to always trust our gut instinct along our spiritual journey.

Other Books by Ozark Mountain Publishing, Inc.

Dolores Cannon
A Soul Remembers Hiroshima
Between Death and Life
Conversations with Nostradamus,
    Volume I, II, III
The Convoluted Universe -Book One,
    Two, Three, Four, Five
The Custodians
Five Lives Remembered
Jesus and the Essenes
Keepers of the Garden
Legacy from the Stars
The Legend of Starcrash
The Search for Hidden Sacred
    Knowledge
They Walked with Jesus
The Three Waves of Volunteers and
    the New Earth
Aron Abrahamsen
Holiday in Heaven
James Ream Adams
Little Steps
Justine Alessi & M. E. McMillan
Rebirth of the Oracle
Kathryn Andries
Cat Baldwin
Divine Gifts of Healing
The Forgiveness Workshop
Penny Barron
The Oracle of UR
Dan Bird
Finding Your Way in the Spiritual Age
Waking Up in the Spiritual Age
Julia Cannon
Soul Speak – The Language of Your
    Body
Ronald Chapman
Seeing True
Jack Churchward

Lifting the Veil on the Lost Continent of
    Mu
The Stone Tablets of Mu
Patrick De Haan
The Alien Handbook
Paulinne Delcour-Min
Spiritual Gold
Holly Ice
Divine Fire
Joanne DiMaggio
Edgar Cayce and the Unfulfilled
    Destiny of Thomas Jefferson
    Reborn
Anthony DeNino
The Power of Giving and Gratitude
Carolyn Greer Daly
Opening to Fullness of Spirit
Anita Holmes
Twidders
Aaron Hoopes
Reconnecting to the Earth
Patricia Irvine
In Light and In Shade
Kevin Killen
Ghosts and Me
Donna Lynn
From Fear to Love
Curt Melliger
Heaven Here on Earth
Where the Weeds Grow
Henry Michaelson
And Jesus Said – A Conversation
Andy Myers
Not Your Average Angel Book
Guy Needler
Avoiding Karma
Beyond the Source – Book 1, Book 2
The History of God

For more information about any of the above titles, soon to be released titles,
or other items in our catalog, write, phone or visit our website:
PO Box 754, Huntsville, AR 72740|479-738-2348/800-935-0045|www.ozarkmt.com

Other Books by Ozark Mountain Publishing, Inc.

The Origin Speaks
The Anne Dialogues
The Curators
Psycho Spiritual Healing
James Nussbaumer
And Then I Knew My Abundance
The Master of Everything
Mastering   Your   Own   Spiritual
    Freedom
Living Your Dram, Not Someone Else's
Gabrielle Orr
Akashic Records: One True Love
Let Miracles Happen
Nikki Pattillo
Children of the Stars
Victoria Pendragon
Sleep Magic
The Sleeping Phoenix
Being In A Body
Charmian Redwood
A New Earth Rising
Coming Home to Lemuria
Richard Rowe
Imagining the Unimaginable
Exploring the Divine Library
Garnet Schulhauser
Dancing on a Stamp
Dancing Forever with Spirit
Dance of Heavenly Bliss
Dance of Eternal Rapture
Dancing with Angels in Heaven
Manuella Stoerzer
Headless Chicken
Annie Stillwater Gray
Education of a Guardian Angel
The Dawn Book
Work of a Guardian Angel

Joys of a Guardian Angel
Blair Styra
Don't Change the Channel
Who Catharted
Natalie Sudman
Application of Impossible Things
L.R. Sumpter
Judy's Story
The Old is New
We Are the Creators
Artur Tradevosyan
Croton
Jim Thomas
Tales from the Trance
Jolene and Jason Tierney
A Quest of Transcendence
Paul Travers
Dancing with the Mountains
Nicholas Vesey
Living the Life-Force
Dennis Wheatley/ Maria Wheatley
The Essential Dowsing Guide
Maria Wheatley
Druidic Soul Star Astrology
Sherry Wilde
The Forgotten Promise
Lyn Willmott
A Small Book of Comfort
Beyond all Boundaries Book 1
Beyond all Boundaries Book 2
Stuart Wilson & Joanna Prentis
Atlantis and the New Consciousness
Beyond Limitations
The Essenes -Children of the Light
The Magdalene Version
Power of the Magdalene

For more information about any of the above titles, soon to be released titles,
or other items in our catalog, write, phone or visit our website:
PO Box 754, Huntsville, AR 72740|479-738-2348/800-935-0045|www.ozarkmt.com

For more information about any of the titles published by Ozark Mountain Publishing, Inc., soon to be released titles, or other items in our catalog, write, phone or visit our website:

Ozark Mountain Publishing, Inc.

PO Box 754

Huntsville, AR 72740

479-738-2348/800-935-0045

www.ozarkmt.com